Hallie's
Secret

Hallie's Secret

by

Carole Gift Page

MOODY PRESS
CHICAGO

The lyrics appearing on page 165 are from "No One Ever
Cared for Me Like Jesus," by Charles F. Weigle, © Copyright 1932 renewal 1959 by Singspiration Music/ASCAP. All
rights reserved. International copyright secured. Used by
permission of The Zondervan Music Group, Nashville.

Library of Congress Cataloging in Publication Data

Page, Carole Gift.
  Hallie's secret.

  Summary: After suffering years of sexual molestation
by her father, thirteen-year-old Hallie has many difficult
adjustments to make in her foster home with a Christian
family.
  [1. Child molesting—Fiction.   2. Incest—Fiction.
3. Foster home care—Fiction.   4. Christian life—Fiction]
I. Title.
PZ7.P137Hal   1987   [Fic]   87-5681
ISBN 0-8024-3476-2

1 2 3 4 5 6 7 Printing/LC/Year 92 91 90 89 88 87

Printed in the United States of America

To you who carry the same painful secret Hallie Shay endured. I do not know your name, but God knows your hurt. Remember, He cares. You are precious in His sight.

Prologue

The first time I saw Hallie Shay, she was standing in my kitchen doorway in a faded jean jacket, tank top, and paisley skirt, her honey-brown hair kind of kinky and free-floating around her face. She was a little wren of a person with a round, elfin face, a clean-scrubbed complexion, and enormous, pale green eyes that glinted with a sad sort of wariness. She was as skinny and gawky as any thirteen year old I'd ever seen.

Frankly, I'd pictured a sophisticated, worldly-wise girl with a shapely body and gobs of make-up. After all, Hallie knew about life—and men—in ways that I, at sixteen, wouldn't experience for years, if ever. You see, Hallie Shay was a sexually abused child. Hallie had come from the Beatrice Crown Home for Girls. My mom and dad, Trish and Kevin Londeree, had agreed to be her foster parents. I, Robin, wanted Hallie to be the younger sister I'd always longed for. Certainly our family had lots of love and faith to share. We practically lived in the church, and we believed God could handle any situation. But none of us realized how Hallie would turn our lives upside-down.

At thirteen, Hallie wasn't a woman yet or a child anymore. She could be a charmer one minute and insufferable the next. I never knew from day to day whether she wanted to be my sister, my best friend, or my worst enemy. Always, it seemed, Hallie Shay was fighting to survive.

I'd like to tell you about Hallie, but I really can't. I haven't been where she's been. I haven't hurt like she hurts. Only Hallie really knows what makes her tick inside. And sometimes I'm not certain that she knows herself. But you'll never know Hallie Shay, or like her, or pray for her unless you hear her story as she lived it—in her very own words.

1

I was lying in bed still as a stone, holding my breath until my chest ached. It was the end of September, two weeks before my fourteenth birthday. The night was heavy with the wet kind of Indian summer heat that makes your pajamas cling miserably to your skin. I kept wanting to breathe, but if I breathed, I might miss a sound—the familiar, warning squeak of the floorboard just outside my bedroom door or the awful click of the doorknob.

Then I heard it—a muffled noise downstairs. Dad was shutting the front door, locking up for the night. He would leave the hall light on for Mom. On Friday nights she worked at Mike's Cafe until midnight. "Tips are good, Hallie," she always said when I asked why she had to work so late. "People get paid on Friday. They don't mind dishing out a little extra."

I hated Friday nights. They were always the same—me waiting alone in my room, lying so stiff my back would ache in the morning, the fear tying little knots in my stomach over and over. Me wondering—*is it going to happen tonight?*

Then, Dad's footsteps on the stairs. My heart did a flip-flop. I closed my eyes and tried to picture myself somewhere far away—maybe on one of those fancy islands with lots of sunshine and sand. Maybe I'd be the only person on the island, and I could run and swim and make sand castles on the beach, and no one would see me; no one would touch me. I'd be free. Totally free.

The doorknob turned.

My heart started pounding like a jackhammer thumping in my ears, filling the whole hot, airless room with its terrible beat. Surely Dad could hear. Surely he would know I was awake. Silently, I begged, *Oh, God—if there is a God—please don't let him touch me tonight!*

I thought for sure my wildly throbbing heart would explode against my ribs. But somehow I managed to lie motionless, my eyes closed, forcing my breath to remain slow and steady.

"Hallie? Hallie, you awake?"

I could sense Dad hovering over me, his big, sturdy frame so close I could feel the dead air stir around me. Even in the dark with my eyes closed I could trace Dad's strong features—his long, straight nose and high forehead, his square-set jaw, his dark eyes shadowed under bushy, close-knit brows.

Mom considered him handsome, always said in her high singsong voice how he looked like some movie star, someone I never heard of, someone who hit the big time maybe twenty years ago, and now maybe the guy was dead or old or long forgotten. I wanted to scream inside my head or hit something hard when Mom started talking about Dad looking like that old movie star. If she thought Dad was so good looking, why didn't she stick around home once in a while? Why did she leave it to me to hold things together and keep peace in the family?

"Hallie, sweetheart? Come on, honey bun, I know you're not asleep." Dad's breath was warm on my cheek. The nauseating smell of booze turned my stomach. Dad must have put away a six-pack while watching the fights. I wanted to turn my head away, but I just pretended I was this still, still statue. *Don't move a muscle, Hallie. Maybe he'll go away.*

"Wake up, Hallie. Your old Dad needs some cheering." His voice sounded whiny and old and helpless. I hated that voice almost as much as I hated his big, booming, angry voice. "It's been a rotten day, baby," he droned on, sounding all beaten down. "I didn't meet my sales quota again. You know what that means—the big boss breathing down my neck. If I lose this job, Hallie, there'll be no more pretty school dresses for you. No more flashy magazines or makeup or soda pop." He nudged my chin playfully. "Come on, honey, let's see my little girl smile for her old man."

I stirred slightly. Couldn't help it. Hated myself already for giving in, for letting him know I was awake. "Please, Dad, please," I groaned. "I'm so tired. Please don't make me do it tonight."

He wouldn't listen.

11

* * *

On Saturday morning, after Mom left for the restaurant, I fixed Dad his favorite breakfast as usual. As he sprinkled pepper on his scrambled eggs, I sat down across from him. My heart was pounding almost as hard as it was last night, but I had to say what had been heavy on my mind for weeks now. "Dad," I said haltingly, "Dad, I been thinking . . ."

He scooped up a mound of eggs on his fork. "Good breakfast, honey. Eggs are just right."

"Thanks, Dad, but listen. I just—"

He looked up. "What's the matter? You need some money? I'm a little short this week, baby, but—"

"No, Dad, it's not money." I squirmed uneasily in my chair. "It's—it's—us."

"Us?" His eyes narrowed. "What about us?"

"You know." I choked out the words. "The messing around. I'm too old for all that now."

Dad's eyes turned hard and dark as he reached across the table for my wrist. "Who you been talking to? I told you never to tell—"

"I didn't, Dad. I promise. It's just that I got other things to think about now."

"You mean boys? You running around with some boy?" When I didn't answer, Dad tightened his grip. "You answer me! Did you let some boy get to you?"

"I'm old enough for a boyfriend," I shot back.

"You think so? Well, I'll tell you, missy. There's no boy that'll treat you better than your

12

old man. And no one who'll love you more than I do. Understand?"

I twisted my hand free and rubbed my sore wrist. "I—I know you love me, Dad," I whimpered, groping for the right words, "but don't you want me to get married someday like other girls?"

Dad pushed his plate away and said grumpily, "Maybe—someday—if I find a guy who's good enough for you. Most of those puny teenage Romeos want only one thing . . ."

Like you, Dad? I wanted to snap. But I held my tongue.

Dad's expression softened. "You aren't thinking of telling on me, are you, honey bun?" His voice was all syrupy sweet again. "You'd get your old dad in a heap of trouble. Like I told you before, I'd lose my job. The police would cart me off to jail, and, well, it would kill your mom. Not that she'd believe you in the first place, but you see how it is, sweetheart. We'd all lose everything we've worked so hard for—our whole happy home. You don't want that any more than I do. Right, honey?"

I bit my lip and stared down at the floor. "No, Dad, I don't ever want anything bad to happen to our family, but—"

"That's why our special way of loving each other has to remain our little secret, Hallie. Promise me again you'll never tell."

I was almost crying now. "I don't want to tell, Dad, but you keep saying you'll stop, and then you don't."

Dad pulled out his handkerchief and blew his nose. "I can't help it, honey. I just love you so much. You just don't know what you do to me."

"I'm sorry," I mumbled. It always turned out like this when I tried to talk to Dad. He made me feel guilty and dirty, like it was all my fault. Maybe it was. Maybe there was something bad about me that made Dad weak. I pushed back my chair and left the table. All my feelings were jumbled up inside. Sometimes I hated Dad for what he was doing to me. Sometimes I hated myself. Sometimes, like right now, I hated us both.

Dad called over his shoulder, "Where you going, Hallie?"

"Nowhere. Just out. Maybe to the video store to rent a movie."

Dad's voice was light and bouncy, like we'd never even just had a serious talk. "Hey, Hallie, rent something with that blonde actress I like—what's-her-name—and we'll watch it together tonight. I'll even order us a jumbo pizza!"

"I don't know, Dad," I mumbled. "Maybe I got plans for tonight."

"Then change them, Hallie. What's more important than spending an evening with your old dad?"

I didn't answer. I just ran out the door, slammed it hard behind me, and ran all the way down the street to Harry's Video Shop where Matt Runyon worked. My Matt. My gorgeous hunk that I was crazy in love with. He would know what to do. He would know how to make the bad feelings go away. He was nineteen and knew every-

14

thing—except the secret I'd promised Dad I'd never tell. But maybe it was time Matt knew. We'd shared everything else. Maybe he could figure out how to make my dad let me go.

As soon as I entered Harry's shop, I spotted Matt behind the cash register ringing up a sale. He looked over, winked, and grinned. I waved guardedly and strolled over to the new releases and pretended to be looking for a movie. But my eyes were still on Matt. I loved the way his coal-black hair curled down his neck and over his ears and the way his lips curved into a tiny little sneer even when he smiled. His eyes were the best—smoky gray like nighttime fog. He could zap you with those eyes. That's what I fell for the first time I met him here at Harry's Video two months ago.

After the customer had gone, Matt sauntered over to me, his thumbs hooked casually on his Levi's. "What's happening, sweet stuff?" he asked in his easy Alabama drawl.

"Nothing, Matt. I just wanted to see you is all."

"Here I am. Looking's free."

"Don't tease me, Matt. I'm not in the mood."

"Yeah? How come? Trouble at home?"

"Yeah—no—I mean, well, it's just that—sometimes my dad bugs me, you know?"

Matt laughed like I'd said something real funny. "Do I know!" he shot back. "When my old man hangs one on, the whole world better watch out! I mean, he gets stinking drunk—"

15

I turned away. My lower lip was trembling, and I didn't want Matt to see. It was always like this when I tried to tell him about my dad. How could I expect him to understand what I couldn't even make myself say out loud to another human being?

Matt came over and spun me around to face him. "What is it, babe? You look like you got big trouble."

"I do," I whispered, fighting back tears.

"Tell me."

"I can't."

"Sure you can. Just say it."

"Not here, Matt. Maybe when I see you tonight."

"What's the matter, Hallie?" He glared hard at me. "You aren't pregnant, are you?"

"No way. It's something else, but I don't want anyone to hear."

"It's OK. Harry's out. Come on in the back room, and I'll get you a Coke from the machine."

I followed him automatically. "I don't want a Coke."

"Suit yourself. I'll have one." He put some coins in the machine and pushed a button. A can clattered down to the opening. He took it, pulled back the ring top, and drank thirstily. Then he wiped his mouth with the back of his hand. "OK, sweet stuff, I'm listening."

I looked up at him. My lips felt dry and stiff. I licked them, but it didn't help.

Matt's cool-guy expression changed. He looked worried.

16

"Hallie, love, you're white as an old spook. What is it? Tell me!"

"My dad—"

"Yeah, he's probably a jerk like my old man, right?"

"No—not like yours," I stammered.

"Sure, he is. Sometimes he drinks too much, sometimes he hits too hard. You just gotta have a tough hide—"

"It's worse, Matt. My dad—he—he—"

The concern in Matt's eyes turned to something else, something that scared me a little. "Say it, Hallie."

I clenched my fists and forced the words out. My voice sounded pinched, hardly there. "My dad—he—he messes around with me sometimes."

Matt's mouth twisted into an ugly snake. "Come on, babe, you trying to gross me out? Are you telling me—you saying he makes you do—what we do?"

I stepped back a little. "I—I been trying to get him to stop since you and me started hanging out together, Matt, but—well, he won't listen—"

Matt slammed the Coke can down hard on the table. Liquid splashed out in a sudden little fountain. "That dirty, no-good—I'll kill him—I swear I'll kill him—!"

"No, Matt, please, don't get mad. It won't do any good. If Dad found out I told you, he'd—"

"How long, babe? How long's he been messing with you?"

"I—I don't know exactly."

"Don't give me that junk. How long? Tell me!"

"Since—since I was—seven."

Without warning, Matt started stomping around the room, slugging at everything in sight, using every cuss word I ever heard. I'd never seen him so blazing angry. For a minute I was more scared of him than I was of my dad. "Man, oh, man, you gotta tell the cops," he stormed. "Boy, let the cops at him!"

I stared at Matt in disbelief. "The police? No way!"

"You gotta, Hallie. It's the only way to stop a psycho like your old man."

"I can't, Matt. My mom would freak out. It would totally wreck our whole family."

"Who says so?" countered Matt. "Your dad? He'll say anything to keep you under his thumb." Matt came over and pulled me into his arms. I looked up into his strong, stubborn face, all my arguments suddenly gone. I felt like I was drowning in his gray, smoldering eyes. "You and me, we really connect, you know, Hallie?" he said, his voice soft as a kiss. "But, angel face, what's mine is mine. I don't share nothing with no other dude, especially your old man. So you gotta choose, Hallie—me or your dad. You can't have us both."

I sank against Matt's chest and sobbed. "I love you, Matt, but I don't know what to do. Please help me. Please, please help me!"

2

From outside, the police station looked like a cement fort with high, small windows and four white columns across the front. I'd seen it before, but I never paid any attention to it, never stopped and really looked at the silent, old building.

I clutched Matt's hand as he steered me inside toward a huge desk where a stern-faced policeman sat. "I can't, Matt," I protested. "I've changed my mind. I'm going to be sick."

"No way, Hallie," Matt countered. "We've come this far. We're putting a stop to your dad's perverted little games tonight."

"I don't want to get Dad in trouble, Matt. Please, I'm so scared!"

Matt put his arm around me. "Don't be scared, angel face. I'm right here with you. I won't leave you."

I looked up pleadingly. "Promise?"

"You bet. Just one thing, babe." Matt lowered his voice to a whisper. "As far as these dudes here are concerned, you and me are just friends, got it? I'm like a—a big brother to you, OK?"

"But why, Matt? I'm proud to be your girl."

"Sure, and I'm proud too, but maybe other folks wouldn't understand, me being nineteen and all, so what we got going is just between us, dig?"

"Yeah, I guess so," I said, not really convinced. But suddenly we were right there at the big desk where the stout, round-faced officer sat staring straight at us. "Hello. I'm Sergeant Brown. Can I help you?" he asked in a deep, husky voice.

"Yes, sir," said Matt, glancing down at me. "Hallie and me—I—we would like to report a—problem."

"A problem?"

Matt nodded. "Yeah, a case of—of child abuse."

The officer's eyes riveted on me. "You, young lady?"

"Uh, yeah."

"Are you hurt?"

"N-no," I stammered. "Nobody beat me up or anything like that."

The officer's voice turned low and gentle. "Then what?"

I shrugged uncomfortably and looked away.

"Her old man," said Matt, barely hiding his anger. "He's been messing around with her."

Sgt. Brown leaned forward. "You mean—sexually?"

"Yeah." Matt's neck vein pulsated. "Yeah, that's it."

"Are you her brother?" asked the officer.

"No," said Matt. "Just a friend. I just found out what's been going on, and I figured the cop—uh, police—should know."

Sgt. Brown studied Matt solemnly. "You're right, young man."

"So what's next?" Matt cracked his knuckles restlessly.

"You file a formal complaint." Sgt. Brown looked over at me and smiled like he actually cared. "Scared?" he asked.

I nodded.

"What's your name?"

"Hallie. Hallie Shay."

His deep voice mellowed. "You did the right thing in coming here, Hallie. We'll make this procedure as painless as we can."

"Will it take very long?" I asked. "I gotta be home by dark to fix my dad's dinner."

Sgt. Brown's smile faded. "It'll take a while, Hallie. I'll have Officer Wallace—a very nice lady—take you to another room. She'll ask you some questions. You just tell her the truth."

"That's all?"

"We'll also need to have a doctor examine you, Hallie."

I trembled a little. "Then I can go home?"

Sgt. Brown's brows lowered, shadowing his eyes. "Not tonight, Hallie."

I felt suddenly like someone had drenched me in a bucket of ice water. I was shivering and cold and weak in the knees all at once. "I told you, I gotta go home," I blurted. "My dad will be wait-

21

ing." I looked up in desperation at Matt, but his face looked just as set and stony as the sergeant's.

Another terrifying thought struck me. "Are you gonna arrest my dad?"

"We'll see, Hallie."

"You can't arrest him!" My voice was coming out all shrill and quivery, like a sob. "He just needs a good talking to, someone to tell him to leave me alone, that's all. He'll listen to someone besides me—I know he will. He'll be good if you tell him to."

"Hallie, that matter will be out of my hands." Sgt. Brown reached across his desk for a pad of paper. "Now may I have your father's name and your full address, please, Hallie?"

"Uh, it's Howard Vernon Shay, and we live at—" Suddenly I couldn't help it. I started bawling like a baby. "Don't hurt him—please don't hurt my dad. Just make him stop. That's all I want. Please just make him stop!"

I felt a gentle hand on my shoulder, and a soft, calm voice said, "Hallie, I'm Officer Wallace. I'd like you to come with me."

I nodded numbly and took one last desperate glance back at Matt. Then I followed Officer Wallace through a giant, crowded office with lots of people sitting at cluttered desks surrounded by metal filing cabinets. The gray walls were cluttered, too, with maps and charts and wanted posters and official-looking papers tacked everywhere. Officer Wallace ushered me into a small cubicle and said, "Sit down, Hallie. Make yourself comfortable. Then you and I will talk."

What happened next is still scrambled in my memory. Maybe I just don't want to remember. Officer Wallace asked me a million questions. Sure, she tried to be nice and polite, even when I described what my dad made me do. But the misery—the hideous shame—was there inside me the whole time, like a balloon blown up in my chest pressing harder and harder against my ribs. I'd never had to put it all into words before. The words made it real in a new kind of way. The more I told, the more I felt like garbage inside, like it was all my fault instead of my dad's.

I'd never felt more lonely and scared in my whole life. Matt wasn't even there to turn to. I wondered why Officer Wallace kept asking me the same things over and over, like she was writing a book or something. Or like she was trying to trick me. Sometimes I wanted to tell her to mind her own business. Then I thought of last night and the desperate, hopeless feeling I had when Dad came into my room again. If I never had to feel that way again, then maybe all the questions were worth it.

It was long past dinner time when we finished. "Can I go home now?" I asked.

Officer Wallace touched my arm lightly and said, "Hallie, have you ever heard of the Beatrice Crown Home for Girls?"

"Isn't that where the orphans live? And maybe bad girls too?"

"It's for girls with family problems, Hallie, girls who need a temporary place to stay until

23

things can be worked out at home. We'll take you there tonight and see that you get a good hot dinner and a nice place to sleep."

A brand new sob formed low in my throat. "But my mom and dad will worry about me."

"We'll call them, Hallie."

"But Matt—"

"We've already sent Matt home, Hallie." She pulled a tissue from the box on the desk and handed it to me. "You know, dear, you've taken the first healthy step toward making things right in your family. It may be a while before you can believe that, but it's true." She smiled kindly. "Now, Hallie, it's our turn to do what we can to start making things right for you."

I nodded, and maybe I said something else. I don't recall now. All I know for sure is that I was walking around in a daze, going through the motions—riding in a police car to the hospital emergency room, enduring the doctor's examination, then later walking up the steps to a sprawling, old-fashioned house and meeting people I didn't want to meet. I said as little as possible and just stared at a plate of something that looked like fish and French fries. I kept thinking that I couldn't swallow anything over the huge lump in my throat, and if I threw up, would they punish me?

Then, finally, a plump, pleasant, rosy-cheeked lady showed me to my bed. I undressed quickly in the dark, pulled on the plain cotton nightgown, and slipped noiselessly between the cool, crisp sheets. My mind was still spinning, like a video tape on fast forward with the action going a mile a minute. Everything was jammed together—the voices, the faces, the feelings. All the faces were twisted and angry, and all the voices were screaming in the silence, and the feelings were like one great ache washing over me.

I tried desperately to think about my fantasy island where I could run free and happy on the windy beach, where no one in the world could find me. But the island was gone—poof!—like a rainbow mirage on the desert. So there I was lying in a strange bed in this big strange room, and all the beds were filled with sleeping strangers. For a long time I lay very still, staring holes in the ceiling. I couldn't cry, couldn't even swallow. I kept thinking, *What have I done? And what are Mom and Dad doing right now? Do they hate me? Will we ever be a family again?*

3

On Sunday afternoon, Mom came to see me at the Beatrice Crown Home for Girls. Anita, one of my roommates—a punk rocker with a purple mohawk and neon green sweater—came and got me. In a confidential drawl, she said, "Come on, geek, move it. Your mom's waiting downstairs in one of the visiting rooms. They wouldn't let her in to see you, so she slipped me ten bucks to come get you. I'm gonna sneak you in and watch the door, so talk fast!"

Anita led me to a private room with a rose-colored sofa and end tables with lots of teen magazines. The windows were covered with heavy red drapes that dragged on the floor. A few lonely slivers of sunshine managed to steal through the high, arched windows.

As soon as I saw Mom's face, I knew she was angry. More than angry. And when she spoke, she reminded me of a hot kettle about to boil over. "They said I couldn't see you, Hallie," she said shrilly. "Can you believe it? My own daughter! But I had to look you in the face, eye to eye, to be sure you hadn't gone berserk or something. And here you are looking sane as you please. Am I the crazy one, or what? My lands, Hallie Shay, you better have some answers. Tell me, what's gotten into you? What in the name of heaven have you done?"

I took a step toward her. "Mom, please—"

"How could you do it, Hallie? How could you hurt your father and me like this? If you were unhappy at home, why didn't you just run away?"

I started to cry. "I—I didn't want to start any trouble, Mom. That's why I never told before. You gotta believe me!"

"Believe you? Believe your filthy lies? You think I'll ever believe another word you say?" She walked over to the far side of the couch and sat down. She rubbed her forehead with both hands like she often did when she had one of her migraine headaches. "If I survive this day," she murmured. "If I can just get through this day!"

"I'm sorry, Mom," I said, sitting down on the opposite end of the sofa. "I'm so, so sorry."

She looked up at me, her face still pinched and strained. "Sorry, you say? If you're really sorry, Hallie, then you march out there and tell these people you were wrong. Tell them you made up this insane story about your dad. We'll go home and try to forget the whole thing."

My tears were coming harder now. "I can't, Mom. It's all true. You—you were always gone— I didn't lie, I swear it!"

Mom flinched slightly and looked away. She sat twisting her purse strap, the same gesture over and over. I knew if it broke, she would be mad at me for that too. "Stop crying, Hallie," she snapped. "Tears aren't going to help matters now."

I fished for a used tissue in my jeans pocket and blew my nose. "Where's Dad?" I asked cautiously.

That set Mom off again. "Where do you think he is, Hallie? He was arrested, carted off to jail like a common criminal. Can you imagine how shocked he was that his own little girl would turn him in?"

I sniffed loudly. "I didn't want them to arrest him. I just wanted them to talk to him. I figured he'd listen to them, Mom."

Mom straightened her shoulders and set her purse aside. "Well, I called our lawyer. Had to get the poor man out of bed early Sunday morning. He's arranging bail for your father right now. If things go as planned, your dad should be home by this evening."

I brightened. "Can I come home too, Mom?"

She looked at me with fire in her eyes. "Are you kidding, Hallie? After the story you concocted, we'll be lucky if they ever let you come home. Don't you understand, daughter? They're making arrangements right now to ship you off to some foster home somewhere. You're going to have to live with strangers, Hallie, until this whole ugly mess is settled."

I started blubbering again, so hard I shook all over. Mom looked startled, then her grim face softened, and she opened her arms awkwardly to me. I scooted over and hugged her tight. I hadn't cried in Mom's arms since I was a little kid falling and scraping my knees on the sidewalk.

"There, there, baby," she soothed as she rubbed my hair back from my forehead. "You've always been such a good girl, Hallie, always minded your mom and dad. You pitched in with the housework when I had to work, cooked your dad's meals, and never gave us any trouble. But I know how it is. When you start growing up, things change. I understand, baby, I really do."

I looked up at her. "Do you, Mom? Do you understand?"

She wiped a tear from my cheek. "Yes, honey, your dad explained it all to me. I know what happened."

A gust of hope soared through me. "He really did tell? Then you know? He told you?"

She patted my hand protectively. "Your dad told me he's suspected for some weeks that you have a boyfriend, Hallie. He said he talked to you about it yesterday morning. He told you you're not allowed to date yet." She held me at arm's length. "Your dad warned you that most teenage boys are out for only one thing, and they don't care who they hurt. My lands, Hallie, you're only thirteen. You're just too young to be involved with boys."

I wiped away my tears with the back of my hand. "Is that all Dad told you?"

Mom cleared her throat uneasily. "He said you were very angry with him. You stormed out of the house and didn't come back. He figured you

30

went to see this boyfriend of yours. Right, Hallie?"

I moved away from Mom and stared at the floor. I studied the swirling flower pattern in the worn, gray rug. "I did go see someone, Mom. A friend."

"Did he put this crazy idea in your head to lie about your father?"

"I—I had to tell someone, Mom. I just had to. He said the police should know—"

Mom stood up and stared at me. Her anger was washing back again like a big wave. "Tell me, Hallie, what kind of creep is this boy to turn a little argument with your father into such a vicious lie?"

I jumped up and faced her. I was trembling. No matter how much air I sucked in, I couldn't catch my breath. "I told you, Mom, it's not a lie!" My words broke in short, halting gasps. "Dad made me do things—awful things! He's been coming to my bedroom for years. He says you—you don't love him enough, that you won't—that you're always too busy. That's why he needs me. Why didn't you—love him more, Mom—so he'd—leave me alone?"

Mom raised her hand and struck me hard across the face, her eyes flaming with rage. "You little tramp! How dare you!" Before I could say a word, she whirled around and stalked out of the room, slamming the door behind her.

I fell apart after that. Not outside. Inside. I wanted to scream. I wanted to run away. I wanted to die. I raced back to my room, threw myself on the bed, and slammed my fists into the mattress. I still couldn't breathe right. My breath and my heartbeat were jumbled because of the giant ache in my chest. Was I having a heart attack? Was this how it felt to die? If I could die right now, I'd never have to face Mom and Dad again. I'd never have to see the hurt and disappointment in their eyes. I'd stop feeling all this guilt and shame. I wouldn't feel anything—just dead. Would it be peaceful to be dead? Or would I go to hell?

My thoughts were interrupted by a light tapping on the door. A pretty blonde lady in a gray business suit peeked in and smiled. "Hallie Shay? Is that you?" she asked politely.

I wanted to come back with a wisecrack like, *I don't have the faintest idea who Hallie Shay is.* Instead I just sat up and nodded.

She came over to me and offered her hand. I ignored it, but she didn't seem to mind. "Hallie, I'm Diana Wilcox."

"So?"

"I'm the social worker assigned to your case."

"The what?"

She repeated the words, then said, "That means I'm here to help you, to see that you're treated fairly and that any decisions made in your behalf are truly best for you. I'm here as your friend."

"I don't need any friends," I mumbled, staring down at my hands. I wondered, *What's this lady's game? What's she after?*

She was still talking on pleasantly, like we were guests at some silly tea party. "I've made all the necessary arrangements, Hallie. Whenever you're ready, I'll be driving you to your foster home."

"My what?"

"You'll be staying with a foster family temporarily, Hallie. It'll be much more pleasant than staying here at Beatrice Crown, although, of course, they do the best they can here. Still, there's no place like a real home."

"I have a real home," I retorted. "Why can't I go there?"

Mrs. Wilcox paused. "Because your father's there, Hallie."

I looked up with a pout. "Why does he get to go home and I don't? Does that mean I'm the one who was bad?"

Mrs. Wilcox gave me a sympathetic smile. "Not at all, Hallie. It's just that, until after the trial, you won't be allowed to stay in the same house with your father. It's for your own protection."

"Trial, you say? They're going to put my dad on trial?"

"You filed a complaint of sexual abuse, Hallie. Your father will likely have to go to court to face the charges you made against him. It's the law. What your father did to you is a serious crime."

I stared at her in astonishment. "Then you believe me? You know I was telling the truth?"

Mrs. Wilcox smiled with her eyes this time. "Of course I believe you, Hallie. I doubt that any girl would have the courage to come forward and do what you've done if she didn't have the strength of the truth on her side."

Somehow, listening to Mrs. Wilcox, I felt a little better inside. Like it was a bit easier to breathe now. Like the hurt had lifted just a fraction off my chest. "Tell me," I said as I stood up and smoothed my jeans, "who is this foster family? And why would they want me?"

4

Just before dusk, Mrs. Wilcox drove me to the suburbs to a white, two-story house with a green, sprawling yard. As we pulled into the driveway, she said, "I think you'll like the Londerees. Mrs. Londeree is a real neat lady. She's taken care of foster children for over ten years."

"So? She gets paid for it, doesn't she?" I snapped. I hadn't planned to sound so sarcastic, but I felt angry, irritated, and scared all in one terrible sensation. I didn't want to meet some strange family, let alone *live* with them! What would they think of me? Would they consider me a troublemaker? A liar? A tramp, like my mother called me earlier today?

"Mr. Londeree is a mechanical engineer," Mrs. Wilcox was saying. "He's a pleasant man with a good sense of humor, a very nice person."

Yeah. I'll bet, I mused silently. *Probably just like my dad.*

Mrs. Wilcox was still chatting on brightly. "Their daughter, Robin, is just about your age, Hallie. Maybe a couple of years older. Mrs. Londeree was very excited when I called and told her about you. She said her daughter has always wanted a sister."

"I'm not her sister!" I uttered coldly. I was digging myself into a dark ditch of resentment, and I couldn't stop. Where was all this hatred coming from? And why did it feel so overwhelming?

"I didn't mean that you had to think of her as your sister, Hallie," said Mrs. Wilcox patiently. "I just thought you might feel more at ease if you knew there was a girl your age in the house, someone who will welcome your friendship."

"What if she doesn't like me?" I asked. "What if I don't like her?"

Mrs. Wilcox smiled. "Why don't we just wait and see, Hallie? Now shall we go in and meet the Londerees?"

I shrugged. "OK. Might as well get it over with."

We both got out of the car and walked up the walk to the big porch. Mrs. Wilcox rang the doorbell. After a minute, the door opened and this pretty, middle-aged lady with short, curly brown hair greeted us. Her eyes were warm and smiling, with long dark lashes. "You must be Hallie," she said, opening the door wide. "I'm Trish Londeree. Come in."

"Hi," I mumbled and followed her inside. I was glad she didn't expect me to shake her hand or anything. Mrs. Wilcox started talking to Mrs. Londeree like they were old friends. I was glad I was out of the spotlight for a minute. It gave me a

36

chance to glance around the house. It wasn't bad —a lot bigger than my house, and the furniture was real nice—not fancy, but you could tell it was expensive stuff.

From where we stood in the living room I could see the kitchen, family room, and dining room. Everything was neat and clean. Or maybe Mrs. Londeree cleaned it just to make a good impression on us. But no; it looked like the place was probably spotless all the time. They'd probably get after me good if I left my stuff around or set a glass on their shiny coffee table. Or maybe they'd put me to work like a maid. Sure, why not? They wouldn't have to pay someone to clean; somebody would be paying them to keep me!

I felt that ugly sensation puffing behind my ribs again—red-hot anger and resentment mingled with a numbing sense of helplessness. Strangers were suddenly dictating every move I made—not my father anymore, or even my mother—but total strangers!

"Hallie. Did you hear me, dear?"

I looked around. Mrs. Londeree was talking to me. "What?"

"I said my daughter, Robin, is looking forward to meeting you. She's upstairs putting the finishing touches on your room."

"My room?"

"Yes, of course, dear. Robin wanted it to be just right—pictures on the wall, fresh flowers in a vase, even just the right records on the stereo." She gave an amused little laugh. "Of course, being sixteen, Robin knows what teenage girls like much better than I do."

She doesn't know what I like, I mused sullenly. *In fact, I bet she doesn't know anything about me!*

"Would you like to come to the kitchen, Hallie?" asked Mrs. Londeree. "I'll show you where things are."

"Yeah, sure." *Scullery duties, here I come!*

The kitchen was light and sunny and smelled yummy, like maybe a cake was baking in the oven. "What do you want me to do?" I asked.

"Do?" Mrs. Londeree looked confused. "I just want to show you where I keep the bread and baked goods and cereals, things like that. We'll have meals at regular hours, but if you get hungry between times, feel free to fix yourself a sandwich or a snack."

"Thanks," I mumbled. Just then I heard quick, light footsteps behind me. I looked around. A girl with long, wheat-colored hair and big, blue, baby doe eyes stood smiling at me, panting to catch her breath. She looked as innocent as an angel, like she'd never had to worry about anything more serious than a hangnail.

"Oh, Hallie—you are Hallie, right? I'm so sorry," she blurted. "I wanted to be at the door to greet you, but your bedspread had a little tear, so I had to sew it, and I'm not the world's greatest seamstress. But I don't think you'll notice unless I point it out."

I shrugged. "I never use a bedspread anyway. They just get messed up."

38

"Oh, well, yes, I know what you mean." The girl's smile was still in place. "I'm Robin. I guess my mom told you about me."

"No, not really." Somehow, the idea of getting acquainted with people like the Londerees struck me as an exhausting, unnecessary task right now. I turned and walked back to the living room where Mrs. Wilcox was waiting. I wondered if she'd consider taking me back to the Beatrice Crown Home. There, in those dozens of identical rooms filled with faceless, identical girls, I could remain anonymous until this whole mess with my dad was over. I wanted to be alone, somewhere where I could sort things out in peace, or else be with Matt. If I could have Matt, I'd never need anybody else.

"Do you want to come see your room now?" Robin was asking from the doorway, her eyes bright with excitement as she nodded toward the stairs.

I looked over at Mrs. Wilcox. She nodded approvingly. The more eager everyone acted, the more bummed I felt inside. But there wasn't much chance Mrs. Wilcox would take me back to the home tonight. She was already standing up to leave. So, OK, I was stuck here. For now, anyway. "Sure." I sighed, following Robin toward the stairs. "Let's see the room."

I had to admit it was a nice room, larger than mine at home, with frilly curtains and real paintings on the walls, not just cardboard prints. There was an oak desk and lamp and an old-fashioned rocker by the window. The bed with its shiny white bedspread was the most beautiful thing I'd ever seen, but I wasn't about to tell Robin. Instead, I pointed to a seam and said, "Is that where you sewed it?"

"Yes," she said, sounding disappointed. "I hoped so much you wouldn't notice."

"What difference does it make?" I snapped. "I'm not the Queen of England; I'm just a girl from the Beatrice Crown Home. You don't have to have things perfect for me."

"But I wanted to," said Robin. "This is the first time my mom's taken in a foster kid I could talk to, someone close to my age. You wouldn't believe the kids we've had here—babies who cried all night, a two-year-old who ate the maple finish off our chair legs, and a three-year-old who walked in his sleep. Once I found him in my neighbor's doghouse, cuddled up next to Fritzy, this big brown bear of a dog—"

"Can I get ready for bed now?"

Robin looked puzzled, hurt. "Already? It's early yet."

"I'm really tired."

"Well, sure; I understand. I put some of my pajamas in the drawer for you, since it'll probably be a few days before your mom sends your stuff over. It's a good thing we're about the same size."

I glanced around. "Where's the bathroom?"

Robin walked over and opened a door. "Right here. We share it. My room's just next door."

"Where do your parents sleep?"

"Oh, their room's down the hall. They have their own bath."

I walked over and checked the bedroom door. It had a lock. I felt better already.

"Do you want anything to eat?" asked Robin. "I make the best popcorn in town."

"No, no thanks." I looked out the door and down the hall, then glanced back at Robin. "Where's your dad?"

"Oh, he's at church. He's an usher. We usually always go on Sunday mornings and evenings, but then Mom and I found out you were coming tonight, so—but we'll all go together next week."

"I don't go to church," I told her.

"You don't? How come?"

"I don't know. I guess my mom and dad never thought it was important."

"Well, you can go with us and see how you like it."

"I don't think so."

Robin frowned slightly. It was the first time she'd let go of that big, bright smile of hers. "I know Mom and Dad will expect you to go to church with us, Hallie. I really think you'll enjoy it."

I was too tired to argue with her, so I walked over to the bed and sat down. I ran my hand over the satin spread. It felt cool and smooth and wonderful.

"Do you have any sisters, Hallie?" Robin asked, sitting down beside me.

"No, I'm an only child."

"Really? Me too! Can you believe it? We're just alike!"

41

I eyed her quizzically. "Are we?" I thought of adding, *Does your dad mess around with you too?*

But Robin was already caught up in the idea of us both being an only child. "Did you ever want a sister, Hallie?" she asked eagerly.

"No, not really." *How would I ever have kept her safe from Dad?*

"Well, I've always wanted a sister," cried Robin. "I even dream about it sometimes, can you imagine?"

I stared at the floor and mused, *I bet your dreams are nothing like my dreams!*

"I know we can't be sisters," Robin was saying, "but I really hope we can be friends, Hallie. I really want you to be happy here."

"Yeah, sure," I mumbled. My ears perked up as I heard a car pull into the driveway, then a sound at the door.

"Oh, my dad's home," said Robin, bounding off the bed. "Come on downstairs, Hallie. I'll introduce you."

I sank back against the headboard. "No, that's OK. You go ahead. I'll meet him tomorrow."

"Oh, Hallie, come on. My dad's terrific. You'll see."

"I'm tired. I'm going to bed," I announced, hugging my pillow against my chest.

Robin walked uncertainly to the door. "Well, OK. I'll see you at breakfast. Sleep well, Hallie."

She went out and shut the door behind her. I scrambled off the bed, ran over and turned the lock firmly. Then I dragged the rocking chair over

42

to the door and propped it against the knob. That should do it, I figured. No one could get in now. No one!

5

When I awoke, the sun was streaming in the window. Everything was bathed in a golden yellow wash. For a minute I felt disoriented. Where was I? Usually the light poured in my window from the other direction. Then I remembered. The whole mess I'd gotten myself into swept over me like a cold, powerful wave. All by myself I'd destroyed my whole family. Now I was being punished—torn from my home and my parents, sent away to live with strangers. Nice strangers, but that didn't matter. They were still strangers. I'd been cut off from my old, familiar life—and from Matt, the only person who really loved me. How would I survive?

I'd survive like I always did—by enduring the bad with the good. That's how I'd lived with my father all these years, gritting my teeth through the bad times and holding on tight to the good times. Yes, there were some good times, like when we played Monopoly together, or watched old westerns on TV, or devoured Big Macs at McDonald's. If only those were my only memories of Dad!

It startled me to realize I was already thinking of Dad in the past, like what happened between us would never happen again. Just thinking about it, I knew I'd rather die than go back to the way things were. So maybe living with the Londerees for a while wouldn't be so bad after all.

I got up and put on my jeans and the Mickey Mouse T-shirt I'd worn the night before. I pushed the rocking chair away from the door, turned the lock, and stepped out into the hall. I smelled bacon cooking. And biscuits. I shuffled down the stairs, my stomach growling with hunger.

I stopped in my tracks just outside the kitchen. What was I supposed to say to these people? How was I supposed to act? I took a cautious step into the room and gazed at the table. Robin was sitting across from her dad. Her mom was serving them breakfast.

"Hello, Hallie," Mrs. Londeree greeted. "Come sit down. We have a place all set for you. Are you hungry?"

"A little," I murmured, dutifully taking my place.

"Hallie, this is my dad," said Robin. "Dad, this is Hallie."

"Hi, Hallie. Glad to meet you."

I gave Mr. Londeree a cautious smile. He had a tan, sturdy face, smiling eyes, and a friendly grin. He looked like he might have been handsome when he was young, but now his sandy brown hair was thinning, and tiny lines were etched around his eyes and mouth. Gentle grooves were carved in his high forehead and lean cheekbones.

"How do you like your eggs, Hallie?" Mrs. Londeree asked.

I looked up in surprise. I couldn't remember anyone ever fixing me eggs before. "I always scramble them," I answered, almost adding, *It's the only way my dad liked them*. Funny. I'd never thought before how I liked them. "No, wait. Fry them instead, so they're still juicy inside."

I was about to reach for the bacon when I realized no one had started eating yet.

"We always ask God's blessing on the food, Hallie," said Mrs. Londeree, sitting down and taking her husband's hand.

I saw then that they were all going to hold hands. I quickly folded mine in my lap and bowed my head politely.

Mr. Londeree's deep voice filled the room. "Lord Jesus, thank You for loving us and taking care of us each day. Thank You for this food and all of Your blessings that You give so freely. Thank You for bringing Hallie to us. Be very close to her in the days ahead. We know life hasn't been easy for her, but we believe You have a divine purpose for her life. We trust You to show her Your love and make the road ahead clear to her. Thank you, Lord. Amen."

I stared across at Mr. Londeree in astonishment. Did he really believe he was talking to God Almighty about me? Did he actually think God cared about a nobody like me—if there was a God? And what was this about a—a divine purpose? Was he spouting some weird sort of hocus-pocus that would put us all in a trance or something? My dad was weird, but I understood his weirdness, or at least was used to it. Mr. Londeree was another matter—speaking to God like it was a common, everyday thing! What was his game? What was he after? And were his wife and daughter as spaced out as he was?

I ate in uneasy silence, wondering if food that was blessed tasted any different. Finally, after my second helping of eggs, Mrs. Londeree announced, "Hallie, I'll be driving you over to Tisdale High this morning to enroll you in ninth grade."

I almost choked. "Enroll me? Are you kidding? I already got a school. I go to Lincoln on the other side of town."

There was a minute of silence before Mr. Londeree said, "While you're staying with us, Hallie, you'll have to attend the school in our district. That's Tisdale High. It's where Robin goes. I think you'll like it."

I looked urgently from one to the other. "You mean I gotta transfer after I just got used to my other school? I gotta start all over again with new classes, new teachers?"

"I'm afraid so, Hallie. Those are the rules—"

"I just can't! I didn't finish my soap project in art or my history report for Mr. Watters. And I'm supposed to be on homeroom cleanup next week—" I stopped abruptly. Here I was jabbering on like some dodo bird. What did the Londerees care about all the changes and interruptions in my life? They didn't know me! Their lives were safe and predictable. Fighting tears, I pushed my chair

48

back and said, "Excuse me. I—I gotta go brush my teeth."

Just as I figured, the whole morning turned out to be one bummer after another. But I didn't argue or cuss or anything while Mrs. Londeree filled out all the papers in the principal's office. I just sat slouched down in the chair with my arms folded tight across my chest and stared out the window. Mr. Benson, the principal, was this wimpy guy who wore goggle glasses and a polka-dot tie and combed his thin hair over a shiny bald spot. When it was time to go, he smiled and stuck out his hand and said, "I'm sure you'll be very happy here at Tisdale High, Hallie. If I can help you in any way, please just stop by my office."

I ignored his hand and turned to the door. "Yeah, sure, thanks," I mumbled. But if he thought I was going to come blabbing to him with my problems, he was one loony dude.

Things went from bad to worse after that. In every class, the teacher introduced me as the new girl in town. In English, Miss Harrison, who was really young and bubbly and pretty for a teacher, asked me to stand up. "This is Hallie Shay," she told the class in her cheeriest voice. "I hope you'll all make her feel welcome."

I forced an awkward little smile and started to sit down. But swell ol' Miss Harrison couldn't leave well enough alone. She had to get downright conversational. "Did your family just move to our city, Hallie?" she asked brightly.

"Uh, no—not exactly."

"Oh, then you're not a stranger to our community?"

"Well, yeah, sort of."

Miss Harrison looked puzzled, but she pressed on anyway in the name of friendliness. "Well, would you like to tell us something about yourself, Hallie?"

"Uh, like what?"

"Well—like—" I could tell that Miss Harrison was winding down, but not soon enough for me. Still smiling, she said, "Oh, you could tell us anything, like where you live, or your hobbies, or what your father does—"

I stared at the floor. My hands were starting to sweat. Miss Harrison would croak if I really told her what my father did.

"Hallie?" she prompted.

"I—I live with the Londerees, Robin Londeree's folks," I blurted. "I—I don't remember the address."

Miss Harrison looked flustered. "Well, how nice, Hallie. Why, I had Robin in class two years ago. A very nice girl—"

I should have kept my big mouth shut, but I could already imagine all the kids thinking, *What's the deal—is she an orphan? Why doesn't she live with her parents?* So I rushed on like a fool and said, "I—I was living with my mom and dad, but they—they had to go out of town—for a while, and—" Everyone was staring at me, waiting, sizing me up, their eyes glazed with disinterest, like they were just daring me to impress them. So I decided to make it good. "My parents had to leave

50

town because—because my dad's a—an ambassador. The President sent him across the ocean to this little country nobody ever heard of, where the people don't even speak English, and their schools aren't that great, so I—well, I stayed here—with the Londerees."

I sat down abruptly and opened my English book. Miss Harrison wisely decided not to pursue the matter any further.

After class a girl stopped me and said, "What's the name of the country?"

I stared at her, baffled, and asked, "What?"

"The country where your dad's an ambassador—what's the name of it?"

"Uh, it's—it's—Bulimia."

"Bulimia?"

"Yeah, it's near—you know—Bulgaria."

"Bulimia's an eating disorder, not a country," scoffed the girl. She whirled around and strutted off like Miss High and Mighty.

"A lot you know!" I shouted after her. I noticed a few of the kids glancing around and snickering, so I ducked into the crowd and made my escape fast.

At noon I joined Robin in the cafeteria line for lunch. It was her idea. She wanted me to meet some of her friends. But I could have gone all day without meeting Zena Pavlik—a tall, funky girl in an oversized, paint-spattered shirt with a ton of fake jewelry. She wore fake nails, plum lipstick, spiked hair, and knee boots.

"Zena's my neighbor," Robin explained as we carried our trays over to a table. "You know, the

51

house on the left, with the dog that looks like a big, brown bear."

"Hi," I said, sitting down. I wasn't in the mood for chitchat, especially after the blunder I'd made in Miss Harrison's class. Talk about pure lunacy—my dad, the ambassador! What a whopper of a lie! Way to go, Hallie Shay!

My ears perked up as I heard Robin telling Zena, "Hallie's a freshman. She's staying with us for a while."

"Oh, really?" Zena tossed me a lazy smile. I managed a tight little grimace back. I was expecting another awkward round of the where-you-from bit, but she just said, "You'll like it at the Londerees'. They're, like, totally nice, you know?"

I nodded and bit into my submarine sandwich. Then I noticed that Robin was just eating yogurt. "You like that stuff?" I asked between hefty bites of cheese and salami.

She made a face. "I'm on a diet."

Zena leaned over confidentially and said, "Robin's into all this yuck-yuck stuff—bean sprouts and carrot sticks and slime milk—" She laughed. "I mean, *skim* milk!"

"It's the price of beauty," Robin lamented in a funny, melodramatic voice. "You see, Hallie, I used to be, well, kinda—"

"She was a real porker," laughed Zena. She elbowed Robin playfully. "A regular chowhound, right, Pudge?"

"Pudge?" I echoed, looking at Robin, all of a size eight, if that.

"That's what the kids used to call me," Robin admitted. "I was a little fatty in grade school."

"Life in the *fat* lane—that was Robin," agreed Zena. "She'd pig out on pizza and tacos and chocolate malts—"

"Yeah, I was a genuine French fry freak—"

Zena reached over and pretended to dip a finger in Robin's yogurt. "You know, Hallie, like, sometimes I think the only way this girl gets nourishment is through intravenous feedings—of strawberry yogurt!"

They both laughed.

I stared from Zena to Robin. "How can you both joke like that about something so—so—"

"It's bigger than both of us," quipped Zena, stifling a chuckle.

"How can we laugh about something so painful, is that what you mean, Hallie?" asked Robin.

"Yeah, I guess so."

Robin smiled. "Well, Zena is my best friend, Hallie. She helped me stick to my diet, and she was always there to encourage me. She never made me feel ashamed or self-conscious about being fat. She just liked me, and accepted me, for myself."

Zena pretended like she was playing a violin, moving her arms in sweeping, exaggerated gestures. "Come off it, Robin. Like, you know, we're drowning poor Hallie in maudlin sentimentality!"

"Don't pay any attention to Zena," Robin told me with a knowing smile. "You'll get used to her after a while."

I finished my sandwich in silence. I couldn't figure these two weirdos out. Were they putting me on or really trying to be friendly? Maybe they were being nice now, but would they laugh at me behind my back? Did Zena know about my dad? Did Robin know? Had the police told anyone? Maybe the whole world knew. Maybe there was something about me that people could tell just by looking at me. Maybe behind their syrupy words and toothpaste grins Robin and Zena were thinking, *This girl let her own father mess around with her. She's nothing but a tramp. She's damaged goods!*

I jumped up from the table and grabbed my tray. My chest felt tight and achy inside, like I couldn't quite catch my breath. "I gotta go," I announced abruptly. "I don't wanna be late to my fifth period class."

"Sure, Hallie," replied Robin. "Zena and I'll meet you after school, OK? We can all walk home together."

I didn't answer. I was already taking long, anxious strides down the crowded cafeteria aisle, helplessly bumping chairs and jostling people's trays. All I knew was that I had to get away, outside, somewhere in the open air, alone, where I could breathe free.

6

I walked home with Robin and Zena after school, mainly because I couldn't remember just how to get back to the Londeree house by myself.

Robin invited Zena and me to join her in the family room for popcorn and diet cola. She wanted to show us her new video of some lady doing aerobic exercises. "Think I can ever learn to do those?" she asked Zena as we watched the incredible contortions on the screen.

"Sure, if you turn into a pretzel," said Zena, wolfing down a fistful of popcorn. She looked at me. "You into aerobics, Hallie?"

"No way. That stuff's boring."

Zena stretched lazily. "Maybe not boring, but definitely exhausting. What we women won't do to look gorgeous for our guys!"

"*Our* guys?" chuckled Robin. "That's what I call total optimism! Just try to tell them they're *our* guys!"

Zena lolled back against the sofa cushion. "Well, I can dream, can't I? Besides, I'll have you know that Roger Cantrell sat and talked to me all through art today. I mean, Robin, he's totally awesome. And, would you believe, he agreed to be my partner for the big semester art project! Now if I can just come up with something cozy for us to do, like building a miniature railroad in his basement or painting each other's portrait. Like, can you imagine anything more romantic?"

"Are you kidding?" exclaimed Robin. She looked over at me. "Does that sound romantic to you, Hallie, building a railroad in some guy's basement?"

"Leave me out of it," I said, wistfully remembering some of my special times with Matt.

"So what's a fun date to you, Hallie?" asked Zena offhandedly.

I could feel the popcorn stick in my throat. "I don't date much," I mumbled.

"Yeah? Well, don't sweat it. You got lots of time. Truth is, I didn't date at your age either."

"You still don't," teased Robin.

Zena tossed a handful of popcorn at Robin. "Well, look who's talking! You think it's a hot date when a guy walks you to your locker!"

"I do not," protested Robin. "But I think it's cool when Darin Chadbourne walks me home from school, which he does whenever he doesn't have football practice."

"Oh, wow, he's totally rad," exclaimed Zena. "Darin Chadbourne is the handsomest hunk at Tisdale High!"

Not as handsome as Matt, I bet, I mused to myself.

"Is he your boyfriend?" I asked Robin, making conversation.

She smiled longingly. "We've dated a few times to church parties and miniature golf, things like that. Nothing serious, but I'm keeping my fingers crossed."

"And your toes, and your eyes," clucked Zena. "He likes you, I know he does, Robin—just the way he says your name and looks at you out of the corner of his eye."

"Maybe, maybe not," mused Robin. "At least he agreed to go with me to the big Sadie Hawkins bash at church a week from Friday."

"Who's Sadie Hawkins?" I asked.

"Sadie Hawkins just means the girls ask the guys," explained Robin. "Our youth group is having a sort of country jamboree, with lots of fiddle music and real barn straw and Southern fried chicken. You're invited too, Hallie. I'm sure there'll be lots of guys and girls there without dates."

"Like me," said Zena. "I just like to play the field—in this case, the ol' corn field. I hear we may even go on a hayride! Have you ever been on a hayride, Hallie?"

I slowly sipped my diet cola. "No, I never have."

"Well, what do you like to do for fun?" Zena persisted.

I shrugged. "I don't know. I never thought much about it."

"I don't mean dating," said Zena, reaching for more popcorn. "I mean, like you and your girl friends. Do you like to swim, or skate, or listen to music, or what?"

"I—I don't have any girl friends," I murmured under my breath. "I'm pretty busy around the house with chores and stuff."

"Oh, wow, that's a bummer," said Zena.

"Don't you have chores?" I asked.

Zena shrugged. "Yeah, like my mom's on my back all the time to clean up my room. I tell her it's cool, like, I know where everything is—"

"I'm sure, Zena," scoffed Robin. "You need a road map to find anything—and a tractor to plow through the junk!"

"All right already, so it's a little cluttered. Maybe I'm just expressing the real me."

"The lazy you." Robin laughed. "My mom makes me clean my room every week whether it needs it or not."

"That's all?" I asked, amazed. "That's all they make you do?"

"No, of course not," said Robin. "I do dishes and dust, stuff like that."

"What about you, Hallie?" said Zena. "What do you do?"

Suddenly—I don't know why—I felt self-conscious. "My mom works long hours, so I'm the only one at home. I cook and clean, you know, take care of the house and my dad—" I hesitated. "At least, I used to, when I lived at home."

"Did your folks die or something?" asked Zena. Then she clapped her hands over her mouth and exclaimed, "I'm sorry, Hallie. I just say whatever comes to my mind. I figured with you living here now and all, that maybe—but I didn't mean to bring up something painful."

I chewed nervously on my lower lip. "My folks aren't dead. They're just—" I thought of repeating the ambassador story I'd told in English, then decided against it. Maybe Robin already knew why I'd come to stay with her family. Maybe she'd told Zena too. Maybe the two of them were baiting me just to be cruel. But no. They seemed friendly enough. Maybe they were just naturally curious.

Before I could think of a reply, Robin stepped in and changed the subject. "So tell us, Hallie," she said, obviously searching for words. "Tell us about—your hobbies. Do you sing, or paint, or jog, or collect things? What are you good at?"

I knew Robin was just trying to make conversation so I wouldn't have to explain to Zena about my folks, but her questions struck another raw nerve. "Nothing," I said sharply. "I'm not good at anything!" But in my ears I could hear my dad saying, *Hey, daughter, you're sure good at making your old man feel better. Nobody's as good as you.*

I jumped up, spilling my bowl of popcorn on the floor, and ran out of the room. I heard Robin calling after me, "Wait, Hallie. We were just trying to get acquainted. Please, don't be upset!"

I ran upstairs to my room, locked the door, and flung myself on the bed and sobbed. Why, oh why, did I always spoil everything! Always mess up, mess up with everybody! Why did I feel so horrible, so totally out of it around Robin and Zena, like I was some sort of alien? Or like I wanted to run and hide? Why couldn't I manage even a silly little conversation? Maybe Robin and Zena really did just want to be friends, and here I acted like a total nerd!

When I'd finally cried all my tears, I sat up on my bed and dried my eyes. Suddenly I realized something important: *I am different. I'm different from Robin and Zena and all the girls at school. I don't feel like they do. I don't think like they do. I'm not even interested in the same things. I know I'm different—terribly different—but do they know? Or is it my secret? Is this one more secret I have to carry like the awful secret about my dad? And, oh, God, is there anyone else on earth who feels the same loneliness and pain I feel?*

7

After school on Tuesday, I found Mrs. Wilcox, the social worker, waiting for me in the Londerees' family room. "I brought your clothes from home," she said, nodding toward two bulging suitcases beside the sofa. I winced a little as I recognized the old, plaid luggage my folks always took up north to Grandma Shay's every summer.

Memories flooded back. I could almost see Dad lugging the suitcases up to the door at Grandma Shay's little farmhouse. She had horses and cows and a million white squawking chickens fluttering around the yard like feather dusters caught in a whirlwind. I liked going to Grandma Shay's even though she and my dad always argued and fought. For some reason Grandma Shay blamed Dad for Grandpa Shay walking out on her, even though Dad was just a little boy at the time. Grandma always reminded Dad that if Grandpa Shay hadn't left, she wouldn't have had to sell most of her land, leaving her practically penniless. Dad always moped around Grandma Shay's with a sullen, hangdog expression, but at least he never laid a hand on me in her house.

"Hallie, did you hear what I said?"

I looked up, startled, at Mrs. Wilcox. "What?"

"You were miles away, dear. I was telling you about your father's arraignment on Friday."

"His what?"

"That's when formal charges will be made against your father in court, Hallie."

"Do I have to go?"

"No, but the district attorney wants to speak to you privately."

"What for?"

"He wants to make sure he has a strong case to prosecute."

"I don't understand."

Worry lines creased Mrs. Wilcox's forehead. "Hallie, in a couple of weeks there will be a preliminary hearing to decide whether there is enough evidence to bring your case before a jury. You'll appear in court and tell the judge your story. Then he'll decide if your dad should stand trial."

"You saying I gotta tell him what my dad did?"

"That's right, Hallie. I know it won't be easy . . ."

I shuffled over and plopped down on the sofa. That old strangled sensation was coming back in my chest. My wrists felt weak and tingly. "You mean that old judge wants to hear all the stuff my dad did to me—all the gory details, everything?"

"I realize it'll be painful, Hallie. I don't like it either, but it's the way our legal system works.

And in the long run your testimony may help your family to work out their problems."

I felt tears sting in my eyes. "Don't give me that. I bet that's just how that dirty old judge gets his kicks!"

"Hallie, it will take courage, I know, but perhaps your testimony will give other abused girls the courage to speak out—"

"I already told the cops everything. They wrote it all down. I saw them. Can't the judge just read that?"

Mrs. Wilcox sat down beside me. She spoke quietly, but her voice was firm. "You're going to have to be strong, Hallie. Strong enough to face your father in court and tell a jury exactly what he did to you. It's the only way justice can be done."

Big tears rolled down my cheeks. "I don't care about justice," I blubbered. "I don't even know what it means. I just wanted my dad to leave me alone. Maybe he will now. But if I keep stirring up trouble, he's gonna hate me—just like my mom does!"

Mrs. Wilcox handed me a Kleenex. "Your mother doesn't hate you, Hallie. Where'd you ever get that idea?"

I blew my nose noisily. I didn't dare tell Mrs. Wilcox about Mom's secret visit to the Beatrice Crown Home. "Mom never liked me much," I mumbled. "She never liked to laugh or hug or play games like Dad did. And now—now that I told on my dad and wrecked everything, I know she hates me."

"Your mother is very worried about you, Hallie. I could tell when I talked to her that she feels very bad about what happened. But I'm sure she just wants what's best for you."

"She doesn't believe me," I muttered. "She thinks I made it all up about my dad because I'm a bad girl." I jumped up off the couch and walked over to the window. I was shaking inside. "I am a bad girl, aren't I, Mrs. Wilcox? That's why bad things happen to me."

Mrs. Wilcox came over behind me and looked out the window too. I thought she was going to put her hand on my shoulder, but she didn't, and I actually felt relieved. She just said softly, "You're not a bad girl, Hallie, and what happened to you is not your fault. I hope someday you can believe that."

"Those are words," I protested, "just words. They don't change anything. They can't change what happened to me or how I feel!"

Mrs. Wilcox was silent a minute. Then she said, "Maybe words can't change things, Hallie, but *you* can change how you feel."

I looked suspiciously at her. "How can I change how I feel?"

Mrs. Wilcox smiled. "One way is to talk to a counselor."

"You mean a shrink? No way! I'm not crazy!"

"No one says you are, Hallie. But a psychologist could help you understand your feelings about yourself—and your dad."

I laughed scornfully. "I don't need a shrink to tell me how I feel about that scum—!"

"Are you so sure, Hallie?"

"Sure I hate my old man? You better believe it!"

This time Mrs. Wilcox touched my arm, so lightly I almost missed it. "Listen, Hallie, would you be willing to see the psychologist if I told you her name is Mrs. Flynn?"

"A lady shrink?"

"That's right."

"Yeah, well, maybe once. This I gotta see—a lady shrink!"

Mrs. Wilcox strolled over to the sofa and picked up her purse. "I have another appointment, Hallie, but there's one more thing—"

"What else?" I groaned.

"There'll be a custody hearing on Thursday. It's just a formality to make it official that you'll be staying with the Londerees until—well, until things are resolved with your father."

"Then I can't go home—not for a long time?"

"I'm sorry. Now that your father's out on bail and back home—"

"Yeah, my dad's back home, and I'm stuck with strangers. It's not fair. Why should he get to go home, and I can't?"

"That's not the court's decision, Hallie."

"Then whose? My mom's? You're saying she wanted him back?"

"It was your parents' decision, Hallie. Your father could have chosen to stay away."

"No, it's my mom," I said bitterly. "She wanted my dad home." I felt a lump form in my throat. "She could have chosen me, couldn't she?

She could have taken me back and made my dad get out, but she wanted him—she believed him—"

Mrs. Wilcox started for the door to the living room, then paused like she was reluctant to go. "It's hard for mothers, too, Hallie—hard for them to accept what's happened."

"Yeah, sure! She blames me, and now she's punishing me," I cried, feeling a sudden spurt of red-hot anger. "But where was she when my dad was fooling around? Why wasn't she there to protect me?"

Mrs. Wilcox looked almost sad. "I don't know, Hallie. That's something your mom is going to have to learn to live with too." She opened the door a crack but still stood watching me. "You know, Hallie, I haven't asked yet how you like living with the Londerees. Are you getting along OK?"

"Yeah, I guess so. They're nice enough. Robin's kind of goody-goody, but I can hack it. She said her mom says I gotta go to church with them. Is that so?"

Mrs. Wilcox smiled. "When you're staying with a family, Hallie, you mind the house rules. It's only fair. But give the Londerees a chance. They're very nice people."

Then why do they want me? I wanted to ask. But no. That would sound like sour grapes. And I did want the Londerees to like me, and Mrs. Wilcox too. Who else could I turn to right now—except Matt? But I hadn't seen or heard from him since he'd taken me to the police station. I'd have to do something about that pronto. Maybe give him a call, make some plans.

"Say, it's OK if I see my old friends, isn't it, Mrs. Wilcox?" I asked offhandedly.

I expected her to say sure, but she looked doubtful. "Friends?"

"You know, like Matt, the guy who helped me turn in my dad."

"Oh, yes. Matt Runyon. He's nineteen, isn't he, Hallie?"

"Yeah, I guess so. He's sort of a—a big brother to me. We just bum around together once in a while—you know."

"Yes, Hallie, I think I understand." Mrs. Wilcox had that frown again. "I'm afraid you won't be able to see Matt for a while, Hallie. It's really best if you don't see your old friends for now."

"Best for who?" I demanded, all my fury mushrooming again. But I swallowed my anger real quick-like. I didn't want Mrs. Wilcox to know how important Matt was to me. Better just to play along, pretend it was OK by me if we were kept apart.

That evening after dinner, while Robin helped her mom with the dishes, I slipped into the family room and telephoned Matt at the video shop. I felt warm all over just hearing his voice again.

"Hey, babe, what happened to you?" he wanted to know. "Why didn't you call? I figured you dropped off the face of the earth."

"I'm calling now, Matt," I told him. "I didn't have any chance before. They took me to that home for girls, you know, and then they brought me here to this foster family clear on the other side of town. They're treating me like a regular orphan, Matt. They even enrolled me in another high school, Te-eas-dale, or something weird like that. I don't know when I'll ever get home again."

"Hey, sugar babe, I wanted to get your old man off your back, not get you shipped off to the boondocks. Why don't you just run away and come live with me?"

"Oh, Matt, I couldn't! How could I?"

"Easy, sweets. I'll just come get you. Can't you sneak out of that holding cell they got you in?"

"It's not that bad, Matt. The people are nice —only—"

"Only they ain't me, right, babe? So like I said, we can shack up together here at my place."

"It's not just *your* place, Matt."

"So OK, I'm sharing this little duplex with a buddy. No sweat. Gordy's cool. He's not gonna make waves."

"Be real, Matt. My dad would be after me in a minute. He freaks out if I look at a guy. If he knew about us, he'd kill you."

"Wanna bet?" Matt shot back. "If that stinking bozo so much as looks your way, the cops'll have him back in the slammer fast."

"Don't call my dad names, Matt!"

"Come off it, Hallie. You oughta hear what I call him when I don't have to clean up my language for your pretty little ears."

"Well, you got what you wanted, Matt," I retorted, feeling suddenly irritated. "Aren't you satisfied? They arrested my dad. Now I gotta go tell the whole world what he did to me. I'm the one who's gotta blab to a bunch of strangers, not you, Matt." A sob rose in my throat. I looked around, fearful that the Londerees might have heard. What would they do if they caught me on the phone with Matt?

"Hallie—Hallie, I'm sorry. I know it's rough, but—"

"I gotta hang up, Matt, before the Londerees catch me. Would you believe, my case worker says I can't see you. What a bummer!"

"Hallie, you'll see me," countered Matt. "I'll pick you up at school at three sharp tomorrow, and we'll go have us some fun, dig?"

8

At noon on Wednesday I joined Robin and Zena in the school cafeteria. It was becoming a regular thing, the three of us eating together, gabbing about boys and classes and boys and homework and boys . . . Of course, they did all the gabbing. I mainly just listened.

At Lincoln High I always took my lunch in a paper bag and ate outside by myself. Dad said it was a waste of money to buy lunch at school when I could pack my own, but after fixing Dad a big breakfast every morning I was usually running late, so I'd just toss a couple of granola bars in my lunch sack.

I hadn't gone to Lincoln High long enough to know anyone very well, but then I've never had many friends anyway. Dad always discouraged me from bringing classmates home from school. He said I had too much work to do, and anything my friends and I had to say could be said at school. I didn't argue with Dad because I didn't want to bring kids home anyway. I was afraid they could tell just by being in our house that something was wrong, that we were different from them. Even now, sitting in the cafeteria with Robin and Zena, I couldn't stop feeling different.

"Hey, Hallie, you've hardly touched your food," Zena remarked, snapping my attention back to the lunchroom. "If your dessert is up for grabs, send it my way. We wouldn't want to tempt Robin with fattening yummies."

"Sure, go ahead," I said, pushing my fudge brownie toward Zena. I figured now would be a good time to approach Robin about my after school date with Matt. I needed her to cover for me. "Listen, Robin," I began cautiously, "I won't be walking home with you today."

"Really? How come?"

"Well, I got other plans. Would you just tell your mom I had to stay late and make up an English test?"

"You've only been here at Tisdale three days and they're already making you stay after school?" exclaimed Zena.

"No, no, it's something else, something personal. I just don't want your mom to worry about me, Robin."

"But if you're asking me to lie, Hallie, I—I can't."

I felt a cold wave of anger wash over me. I thought, *I bet if Zena asked you to lie, you would!* I wasn't about to make a scene here in the cafeteria, so I just stood up and whisked my tray off the table. "Well, Robin, if your mom asks where I am, will you at least keep your mouth shut about what I just told you?"

"Wait, Hallie. Tell me where you're going. Maybe I can help."

"Yeah, sure. I can see right now you'd be a big help. Thanks for nothing!" I stalked away, angry with Robin and myself as well. Why had I even told her I had plans for after school? And why did I ever think she'd take my side?

After my last class I hurried outside, then waited almost twenty minutes beside the curb before I spotted Matt's old, dented, gray Mustang roaring up the street toward me. He swerved over, and I hopped in beside him. I'd never felt so happy to see anyone in my life. He pulled me against him and kissed me right in broad daylight. My heart was singing like crazy. I was Matt's girl, and he didn't care who knew it.

He drove across town to my old neighborhood and stopped at a liquor store for a six-pack, some diet cola, and a bag of chips. Then we headed for his little duplex just two blocks from the video shop.

I was disappointed to see that Gordy was home, slouched in front of the TV with a can of beer. I'd hoped Matt and I could be alone. Besides, I didn't like Gordy. He always looked at me with his leering, weaselly eyes and made crude remarks when Matt was out of earshot. I guess I was a little afraid of Gordy too. I had a feeling he was just waiting for his chance to make a pass. But then, weren't all guys like that anyway?

"Pour yourself some cola, babe," Matt was saying. He already had himself a beer and was sitting down in the old, overstuffed chair. He patted his knee. "Come sit here, Hallie, and we'll get nice and cozy."

I looked doubtfully at Gordy. He had straggly, greasy hair and a scrawny face with a thin mustache that reminded me of mouse whiskers. "I can't stay long," I stammered.

"Sure you can," said Gordy. He got up and sauntered over close to me. "Ol' Gordy's got business to tend to, so you just stay as long as you like." He grinned and pinched my leg. I felt like kneeing him back, but I didn't want to start any trouble. Matt always looked up to Gordy like he was the coolest thing on two legs.

After Gordy left, I felt a little more relaxed. Matt and I watched an old "Bonanza" rerun on TV. Then he started getting real kissy and wanted to head for the bedroom.

"Not this time, Matt," I told him. "I gotta get back to the Londerees' before dinner, or they might get mad and send me back to that old girls' home."

Matt held me tighter. "Come on, angel face, I didn't bring you over here just to watch TV."

I struggled free. "I mean it, Matt. I gotta get back now."

Matt stood up grudgingly and twirled his car keys on his finger. "I said you could move in here, sweets. Just say the word."

I slipped into his arms again and choked out the words. "Oh, Matt, I want to be with you so much. You're the only one I can trust, the only one in the world who cares about me."

"I'm crazy about you too, sweet stuff, so what's the—?"

"But I can't move in with you, Matt, not yet. My life's all messed up right now, with my dad and the trial and all. I gotta get my head on straight first." I searched his eyes, breathless, my heart pounding. "You will wait for me, won't you? I'm still your girl, right?"

"Yeah, sure. You'll always be my girl, Hallie. I'll bash in anyone who tries to keep us apart."

With little more argument, Matt drove me back to the Londerees', letting me out a block from the house. I ran the rest of the way and burst in the door just as everyone was sitting down for dinner. They all looked at me like I'd been gone a week.

"Hallie, where were you?" exclaimed Mrs. Londeree. "I was about to telephone Mrs. Wilcox."

I quietly took my place at the table. I could tell that Mr. Londeree was about to question me too, so I promptly bowed my head. He took a deep breath and prayed. I hoped by the time grace was over, he'd be thinking of something else besides me. But no such luck.

"Now tell us where you were, Hallie," Mr. Londeree persisted. His usual pleasant face was marred with frown lines.

I reached for the mashed potatoes.

"We're waiting for an explanation, Hallie," he declared.

I forced my voice to sound as casual and sincere as possible. "I was at school making up an

English test. Miss Harrison gave it to the class last week before I came here to school." I looked up plaintively at Mrs. Londeree. "Miss Harrison said I wouldn't be so far behind if I took the test today."

"But, dear, why didn't you let us know?"

"I did! I told Robin at lunch that I'd be late. Didn't she tell you?" I gazed silently at Robin, daring her to contradict me.

"Robin, is that true?" asked Mrs. Londeree.

Robin and I stared each other down for a long minute. I could tell she was getting real uneasy. Finally, she mumbled, "I guess Hallie said something at lunch about staying late for an English test, but I can't remember exactly what she said."

"Robin, dear, that's not like you to be irresponsible," said Mr. Londeree. "You could have saved your mother and me some worry if you'd just told us about Hallie's test."

"It won't happen again, Dad," she murmured, her eyes downcast.

I helped myself to the roast beef and gravy. I was careful not to glance at Robin again for the rest of the meal.

That evening, just before bedtime, Robin knocked at my door. I quickly moved the rocking chair away and flicked the lock open. I didn't want Robin and her folks knowing I propped the rocker against my door every night. It wasn't any of their business anyway. It was just a little precaution.

Robin strode right in and sat down on my bed. I could tell by the glint in her eyes that she was angry. "Hallie," she blurted, "that was a dirty

76

trick you pulled. I don't appreciate you forcing me to lie to my parents."

I tried to sound cool and unconcerned. "Then why did you?"

"You trapped me into it. You knew if I didn't back you up you'd be in deep trouble. They might have sent you back to Beatrice Crown. You knew that and were just counting on me to feel sorry for you."

I glared her down. "I don't ask anybody to feel sorry for me!"

"Well, don't ask me to lie for you either, because I won't do it again."

I stared in amazement at Robin. She was actually ready to cry. "It's no big deal," I told her matter-of-factly. "Just a little white lie. Nobody got hurt."

Robin stood up and walked to the door. "Maybe lying isn't a big deal to you, Hallie, but it is to me. My parents trust me, and I don't ever want to do anything to destroy that trust."

"Trust? What's trust?" I countered, suddenly irritated by Robin's syrupy, pie-in-the-sky prattle. "Trust is just a dumb word. I don't think there's such a thing as trust!"

Robin looked me straight in the eye, not angrily, but as frank as any look I'd ever seen. "You've got a lot to learn, Hallie," she said softly. "I just pray to God you'll give Him a chance to help you someday."

"Who says I need any help?" I shot back bitterly, edging her out the door. "I'm no little kid, you know. I could tell you and your giggly friend

Zena some things that would shock you right out of your eyeballs. I may be only thirteen, but I'm older than the two of you put together!"

9

I knew I'd blown it with Robin. She acted all icy cool and reserved at the breakfast table the next morning. I couldn't stand the idea of her looking down her nose at me, so I deliberately upset the milk pitcher. It spilled onto her plate and ran down onto her lap. She shrieked and jumped up and ran to the bathroom. I was laughing inside, but I put on a real sad face and apologized all over the place to Mr. and Mrs. Londeree. They both told me not to worry; it was just an accident. But I could tell that the meal was spoiled anyway, and I was glad when it was time to leave for school.

Mrs. Londeree picked me up early that afternoon for the custody hearing. We drove downtown to this massive old courthouse with lots of fancy trim. In the yard stood a big stone statue of a half-naked lady holding up some scales. The sign on the pedestal said, "Justice." I figured that was another one of those words, like "trust," that people threw around without any idea what it meant.

The custody hearing was short. My mom was there, but she didn't even look at me or speak to me. The judge talked in a flat, droning voice, like maybe he was half asleep or else bored silly with the whole mess. It was all predictable stuff: I would be staying with the Londerees for what the judge called "an indeterminate time." Mom didn't even offer a word of protest.

On Friday I had to miss classes again. Mrs. Londeree drove me to an office building downtown and introduced me to a stodgy-looking man named Andrew Stone. Mr. Stone was my court-appointed attorney. He explained that he would be the prosecuting attorney if my case went to trial. I figured that meant him and me against my dad. He wanted me to tell him everything that had happened, only he wanted specific dates and times, and he kept saying how important it was to be absolutely accurate. Like, what were my dad and I wearing at the time of the alleged abuse and what was the weather like? What did we have to eat? What was playing on the radio? Crazy stuff like that.

I started feeling real angry inside. What did this jerk lawyer think I was gonna do—keep a diary of everything? For sure! Like, *At 10:15 P.M. on December 6, my dad came to my room in his maroon bathrobe, and it was snowing outside, and there was ice on the window, and I was wearing my flannel pajamas that Grandma Shay gave me, and Madonna was singing on the radio, and a fly was walking across the ceiling* . . .

Man, what kind of idiot did he think I was? I always did all I could to blot those ugly times out of my mind. I was on my fantasy island lying on a warm, sunny beach or swimming in crystal-cool water, anywhere except there with my dad. Sometimes I even pretended I was someone else and that it wasn't me with my father, not the real me, not the part of me that mattered. I got so I was real good at pretending I was someone else, or somewhere else. I could check right out of my head real fast when I had to.

I didn't tell the lawyer much of anything that afternoon. I could see he was getting miffed. "I need facts, Hallie," he kept saying. "I need verifiable facts if we're going to put your dad where he belongs."

Where does he belong? I wondered. *How can a stranger know where my dad belongs when I don't even know?*

That same afternoon, Mrs. Londeree drove me to the courthouse to see the district attorney. Mr. Kaufman was a short, bald man with a middle-age paunch, and when he walked he reminded me of a squat, little penguin. But he had a nice deep voice. If I closed my eyes when he talked, I could picture a tall, handsome man. I wondered if it bothered him, having such a great voice and looking so ordinary.

"Miss Shay, why do I have the feeling that you're not listening to me?" he asked from behind his wide, wide desk.

"I'm sorry," I mumbled. For a minute we just sat staring at each other. I wondered if *he* had any little girls, or any secrets.

"Miss Shay, do you know why you're here?"

"No."

He looked startled. "Didn't Mr. Stone explain the legal procedures you would be involved in in the days to come?"

"Maybe. I don't remember."

"Did Mr. Stone tell you about the preliminary hearing?"

"I—I guess so."

"You'll be called on to testify against your father, Miss Shay. You and I need to talk about what you're going to say."

I sat back in my chair and sighed. "Does this mean I gotta tell you the whole thing about my dad just like I told the lawyer?"

"That's right, Miss Shay."

"And then I gotta say it again at this—this preliminary hearing?"

"Yes, that's the procedure."

I sat forward and clutched the chair arms. "And then I gotta blab it all again at the trial?"

"I know it won't be easy, Miss Shay. These things never—"

"I changed my mind."

"What? What did you say?"

"I said, I changed my mind!" My voice was suddenly coming out all loud and shrill. I couldn't control it. "I don't want to prosecute my dad. Maybe he'll be good, now that everybody knows, or maybe I can stay awhile at the Londerees', or I got a terrific friend I could stay with by the video shop—"

"Miss Shay, you don't understand. You've already reported the crime. You can't drop the charges now. This matter can only be handled through the court system. You simply must testify."

I started to bawl. That shook Mr. Kaufman up. He called in his secretary, and she took me to her desk and gave me some Coke in a paper cup. Then she handed me a *Newsweek* magazine and told me to sit down and compose myself. But a half hour later I was back in Mr. Kaufman's office, and I had to tell him all the garbage about me and my dad after all.

I was glad when the weekend arrived. I didn't have to go to school or talk to any more lawyers or D.A.'s. I could sleep in and dream about my tropical island.

On Saturday afternoon Robin and I helped Mr. Londeree clean the basement. It was interesting to see all the junk people collect over the years—old yearbooks, dusty packets of letters, faded photographs of people in funny, antique clothes, and tons of hilarious knickknacks and useless gismos. Robin and I sat on the stairs and looked at the pictures and laughed till our sides nearly split. She was friendly and bubbly again, just like at first, and I decided I liked her too. I was even feeling a little sorry I'd made her lie for me.

Then Robin found some mushy love letters her dad wrote her mom before they were married. We started reading them, and they sounded really romantic, like what Rhett Butler would say to Scarlett O'Hara in *Gone with the Wind*—not dirty, but real passionate, like he loved her more than anything in the world and would even die for her. The letters were just getting good when Robin put them away and said they were private, and maybe we shouldn't be reading them.

"I never knew real people felt that way," I said. "I thought that kind of love was just made up in books."

"My folks are still in love," said Robin. "I've heard them tell each other lots of times."

"That's cool." I could see it was something Robin was proud of, but I figured that kind of love was about as real as my fantasy island. But I wasn't about to tell Robin there was no such thing as true love; she'd find it out soon enough.

On Sunday morning I went to church with the Londerees. I didn't really want to go. I couldn't remember ever being in a church before, and I didn't know what to expect. Would it be all quiet and solemn like a funeral? I'd never been to a funeral either, but the thought of one gave me the creeps.

I was surprised to see that the church auditorium was pleasant and sunny, with comfortable seats and modern furniture. And the people weren't all grim and sour-faced after all. Before the service started, everyone was talking and laughing and greeting one another like it was a neighborhood barbecue. The Londerees introduced me around, and then we all sat down right up at the front. I scooted down in my chair, especially after a while when the preacher started talking about people confessing their sins and asking for God's forgiveness. I knew for certain Mr. Londeree must have put a bug in the preacher's ear about me because that Holy Joe was talking right at me, telling me I needed to come to Jesus.

I tried to hide behind the hymn book, but that minister's eyes were drilling right through me. I had a feeling that everybody in the place knew the preacher was talking right at me. Was it possible the Londerees had told their whole church about me?

I heaved a big sigh when the whole thing was over and we all filed out. But they weren't finished with me yet. Robin announced brightly that I would be going with her to Sunday school.

"Then what was that we just came from?" I asked.

"Church."

"You're telling me there's more?"

"Sure. In Sunday school we get together with kids our own age. Just come on and try it, Hallie. You'll like it!"

I followed along dutifully, but I felt more on exhibit than ever in this little room with maybe twenty high schoolers. When I realized our teacher was this handsome college jock named Jerry, I figured maybe it wouldn't be so bad after all. But pretty soon he started talking about how our bodies are the temple of the Holy Spirit, so we should honor them and take care of them and all. He started in on drinking alcohol and smoking and taking drugs, explaining how all that stuff harms us and keeps us from being what God wants us to be.

Then he began talking about sex and how God meant it to be a beautiful expression of love between a husband and wife. I perked up my ears real quick, because if there was one thing I wanted to know, it was how God and sex could have anything in common.

Jerry's voice really boomed in the little room. "The more sacred something is to God, the more Satan perverts and distorts it," he declared. "Satan can't create anything good or worthwhile. All he can do is destroy the good things God has made. So he twisted people's minds about sex. He made them misuse it and abuse it and misuse and abuse other people in sexual ways."

When I heard that, I did a double-take. Had the Londerees told *everyone* about me? Was Jerry going to point me out and use me as an example of the devil's work? My heart started pounding hard, and my hands grew clammy. I could feel little beads of sweat forming on my upper lip.

I could tell Jerry was on a real roll now. "One of Satan's greatest victories is the way he makes people think of sex as something dirty and unclean," he said. "When we think of the word *sex* we don't think first of God. We think of risqué ads or four-letter words or porno movies. We associate sex with evil things. But God didn't create sex to be evil. He created it as a beautiful form of communication between a man and a woman, to represent their oneness in marriage before God. He never meant it to be a casual form of recreation."

Jerry paused, letting his words hang in the air for a minute. Then it seemed he looked right at me and said, "Sex is such a powerful force in our lives that when it's misused it affects every part of our personalities. It makes us feel guilty and ashamed—"

I leaned over and elbowed Robin and whispered hotly, "Why did you tell him about me?"

She stared at me in surprise. "What are you talking about? He doesn't have the slightest idea who you are."

I didn't believe her. "I gotta go to the bathroom," I whispered and darted out the door as fast as I could. I ran all the way down the hall, just in case that Jerry guy decided to come after me. I couldn't get over it. The whole church must have been warned that I was coming. No one, no one in the world, would let me forget the shame I felt. If I couldn't get away from my guilt feelings even in a place full of strangers—a church, in fact—then what hope did I have? I might as well be dead!

That thought startled me. Not because I hadn't thought of it before, but because of how easy it came to me and how reasonable it sounded. Not like something to be afraid of but like something welcome and familiar. Maybe death was like my fantasy island. Whatever death was like, at least it would stop the guilt and pain.

I looked around for a telephone. If I could just call Matt, I'd feel better. He would say something funny and cheer me up. At last I found a pay phone in an empty hallway. I deposited my coins and dialed with trembling fingers. I waited as Matt's phone rang and rang. Bonkers! No answer. He and Gordy were probably out scavenging around. I didn't trust Gordy. I never knew what scam he was into next or what trouble he'd get Matt into.

I hung up the phone and trudged down the hallway. Now what? I wanted to die. But how? I walked aimlessly, looking for the church exit. Then I heard singing coming from somewhere down the hall, so I followed the sound. I came to an open door and peeked in. A bunch of little kids were sitting in a circle singing a song I'd heard somewhere before, a long time ago.

> Jesus loves me, this I know,
> for the Bible tells me so . . .

I leaned against the wall and listened. I closed my eyes and pretended I was one of those little kids singing their hearts out. And for the first time in my life I wished I could believe in a wonderful God who could make everything right and beautiful and clean.

I don't know how long I stood there listening to those kids sing, but suddenly there was a rustling sound, and all the boys and girls came scrambling out, laughing and shouting and bumping one another in their eagerness to be off and running. I waited until the hall was clear again before I made my way out of the church to the Londerees' car. But all the way the sweet, happy words of those innocent little boys and girls kept ringing in my ears, *Jesus loves me, this I know* . . .

10

On Sunday afternoon the Londerees took Robin and me to a nearby park for a picnic.

"This will probably be our last picnic of the season," Mrs. Londeree told us as we spread a checkered oilcloth on the rustic log table. "Can you believe it's autumn—the leaves turning color, the air growing brisk? Don't you girls think there's something bittersweet about the last picnic of the year?"

I nodded like I knew just what she meant. I didn't tell her this was my *first* picnic ever, that I couldn't remember my folks ever taking me on a picnic. Dad would have considered it frivolous; Mom would have hated the ants and inconvenience. When I was a kid, whenever I teased Mom to take me somewhere fun, she always said it took all her energy just to survive. "Just wait until you're an adult, Hallie, and have to carry heavy trays of food till all hours and serve rude, rowdy customers. Then see if you feel like running around to zoos and movies and amusement parks."

Sometimes Dad would take me to the carnival or the ice cream parlor, but I always knew what price I'd have to pay, so after a while I stopped asking him to take me places.

Mrs. Londeree handed me a big cardboard bucket of steaming fried chicken. "Would you set it on the table, Hallie? And there's potato salad and baked beans in the wicker basket."

Robin and I set the table, placing paper napkins under the plastic plates so they wouldn't blow away. Mr. Londeree poured cups of Kool-Aid from the big thermos jug. Then we all sat down and bowed our heads for grace. They held hands as usual, but I kept mine folded tightly in my lap. Somehow I just couldn't make myself reach out and let someone hold my hands. Just thinking about it made me lose my breath a little, like maybe they'd hold too tight and not let go.

The picnic lunch was terrific. The hot, crispy chicken tasted even better in the fresh air. After we'd eaten and cleaned up the mess, Robin and I walked to the playground and sat on the swings.

"You know, I don't think I'll ever outgrow swings," Robin said as she drew back and let herself soar into the air. "Don't you agree, Hallie?"

"Never thought about it." I pushed off too and felt the cool air cut across my bare legs as I swung skyward. I could imagine myself flying clear up into the fleecy white clouds and bouncing like a rubber ball in those big, billowy cotton fields.

Robin looked over and laughed giddily. "When I was a kid, I'd swing as high as I could and then jump out like a dive bomber. My mother used to have a fit. Said I'd break a leg. I never did."

"How come your parents are so overprotective?" I asked.

"I don't know," said Robin. "I guess they just care."

After a while we slowed down and coasted a little and caught our breath. Robin's expression grew thoughtful. "I got the feeling you didn't care much for church, Hallie."

"Not much."

"How come?"

"I don't know. I just felt sort of—uncomfortable."

"Did you really think I told my Sunday school teacher about you?"

"Yeah—the way he was talking."

"I didn't, Hallie. I didn't know anything to tell him."

"Sure you did. I bet your folks filled you in plenty on me."

"No, Hallie. They just said—your dad abused you."

"Did they tell you how?"

"They said it was—sexual abuse, but that's all they told me, honest."

I dug the toe of my tennis shoe into the dirt. "I bet you're real curious, aren't you? I bet you'd like to hear all about it."

"No, not really. I—I can't even imagine such a thing."

I glanced over at her. "I guess your life has been a piece of cake compared to mine, huh?"

"No, not really, Hallie. I mean, it probably hasn't been nearly as traumatic as yours, but I—I've had some battles to fight too."

"You're kidding! Your folks seem about as mellow as pudding."

"Oh, my parents weren't my problem. I guess in a way I was my own worst enemy."

"I don't get it. How could you be your own enemy?"

Robin swung slowly now. "Well, when I was six, I was this little fatso kid with chocolate bars sticking out of my pockets. I'd pig out on jelly donuts for breakfast, then sneak candy to school and devour it during recess. The kids used to tease me a lot. They'd call me 'laundry basket' and make jokes about my dirty laundry."

"Why 'laundry basket'?" I asked.

"Because of my last name—Londeree. It sounds like laundry. Once a chocolate bar melted through my jeans pocket, and the kids sang this dumb little chant telling me to go home and wash my dirty laundry. I was totally mortified."

"Kids can be real jerks," I murmured.

Robin brought her swing to a standstill. "Yeah, well, anyway, I was a real loner all through grade school. I couldn't imagine anyone liking me—except for Zena, my next door neighbor."

"So Zena was your neighbor even back then?"

"She sure was—and my best friend too. She stuck by me through thick and thin—literally. By junior high she persuaded me to trade my chocolate bars for lowfat yogurt and convinced me that jogging had it over bingeing any day."

"And that did the trick, huh?"

Robin chuckled. "Well, that was a start. It took a few more years for me to slim down and trade my awkwardness for a small measure of grace. Actually, I'm still working on it. In fact, I guess it's something I'll have to work at all my life."

"You mean, like, no more chocolate bars and fattening stuff?"

"You got it!" laughed Robin. "And that's not always so easy, especially when my mom gets on one of her baking sprees."

I nodded. "Yeah, your mom's a great cook."

Robin looked over at me. "Hallie, I—I just wanted to say—well, I'm sorry I got mad at you the other day—"

I stared at the ground. "You mean for making you cover for me?"

"Yes. Lying was wrong, but I was wrong to snub you like I did."

"No big deal."

"It was to me, Hallie," said Robin. "You know, I really do want us to be friends."

"Friends? Yeah, sure. That's cool."

Suddenly we heard a shout and looked around. It was Robin's dad striding toward us, grinning. He was a lean, lanky man, but he ran like an athlete. Even through his polo shirt, his arms and shoulders looked like solid muscle. He was smaller than my dad but in much better shape.

"Hey, you girls going to swing all day, or you want to hike with me up Carver's Hill?"

"Climb Carver's Hill?" cried Robin. "Through all the rocks and weeds?"

"Aw, come on, you're an old softie," scoffed Mr. Londeree. "Why, I used to climb mountains when I was your age!"

Robin laughed. "Sure, Dad, and you walked ten miles to school through blinding snowstorms!"

"Five miles. Anyway, you girls joining me or not?"

Robin looked at me. "I'm game if you are, Hallie."

"I don't know. I guess if you want to." Robin sprang out of her swing and bounded after her dad toward the grassy, jutting hill in the distance. I followed too, a few steps behind. It wasn't very steep, but it was uneven and rocky, with spiky bushes everywhere. We hiked for almost an hour and were still only halfway to the top.

"Really, Dad, this isn't my idea of fun," Robin finally called breathlessly. She was a good dozen feet behind her dad and me now and falling farther behind with every step.

I was tired too, but I felt a strange sense of exhilaration as I scaled the rolling, scrubby hill beside Robin's dad. Somehow, I wanted to prove to him that I was better, faster than his own daughter. It was like a personal, unspoken challenge to see if I could keep up, keep pace with him. Just then he looked back at Robin and shouted, "Come on, kiddo! Look at Hallie here. She's a regular little trooper!"

A regular little trooper! The words tingled inside me. Robin's dad thought I was OK. I was a trooper. It was a good thing to be.

Summoning all the energy I had, I sprinted forward with a new burst of speed. *Look at me, look at me!* I wanted to sing. Then it happened. My right foot grazed a jagged rock and twisted with a sudden lightning bolt of pain. I went down, sprawling like a rag doll into the dry, weedy thicket. I uttered a raw, shrill scream and doubled up in a ball, nursing my throbbing ankle.

Robin's dad darted to my side, knelt down, and reached for my ankle. I drew back instinctively, recoiling at his touch.

"It may be broken, Hallie," he warned. "Better not walk on it."

"But I gotta," I moaned. Awkwardly I hoisted myself up with my hands and put a little pressure on my foot. The pain was searing. I crumpled back down on the ground.

"Please, Hallie, let me help you," said Mr. Londeree.

"I can do it myself," I insisted. "I'll scoot downhill on my behind if I have to." I scudded along the rough ground a few feet, then gave up. My ankle was swelling rapidly. I was in agony.

"It's OK, Hallie," said Mr. Londeree as he gathered me up in his arms. "Hold on. I'll carry you back to the picnic area. There's a first-aid kit in the car."

I was about to protest some more, but then I realized nobody had ever carried me in their arms before. At least, not that I remembered. Suddenly, instead of feeling tense and terrified, I felt all warm and safe and protected. Like a baby. I put my head against Mr. Londeree's chest and closed my eyes. In my mind I pretended like I was a helpless little baby again who couldn't even walk or talk, who couldn't do anything at all but be loved and held. It was the best feeling in the whole world. I wanted to stay in Mr. Londeree's arms like this forever.

11

The Londerees drove me immediately to the emergency center where a doctor examined my bruised, swollen ankle. "Well, young lady," he said, "you're lucky the ligaments weren't torn. You rest that ankle and keep it elevated a few days, and it'll be good as new."

"When can I walk on it?" I asked.

"Maybe a week. Depends on how it feels."

"But what about school?"

"Crutches can get you wherever you need to go."

"Crutches? Oh, yuck!"

I stayed home from school for the next two days nursing my sprained ankle. Each morning Mr. Londeree carried me downstairs to the family room sofa, and Mrs. Londeree fluffed a pillow for my head and brought me my meals on a TV tray. I lazed around all day snacking and watching game shows and soaps. I couldn't remember anyone ever waiting on me like this in my whole life. It was terrific. I felt like a baby being pampered and spoiled. I pretended like I couldn't even walk or talk yet, like I was this helpless, innocent little kid who didn't know anything yet and couldn't do anything for herself.

But after a while I could see that Mrs. Londeree was getting a little irritated. "Hallie, dear, I don't think you're quite as helpless as you're acting. You do nothing but watch TV. And for two days you've hardly said more than baby talk. I really don't think a sprained ankle should affect your speech."

"I *am* a baby," I snapped. It was a dumb thing to say, but it was the only thing I could think of. It was how I felt right now.

"Well, tomorrow you're going to use your crutches and go back to school."

"I hate school," I mumbled under my breath. "Nobody likes me."

"Well, they will like you, Hallie, if you give them a chance." Mrs. Londeree eyed me carefully. "You do know that Robin and Mr. Londeree and I like you, don't you?"

"I—I guess so." I thought about Mr. Londeree. Yes, he seemed to like me. He had carried me all the way back to the car when I sprained my ankle. Every day he asked how I was feeling. He was always very nice and polite, like he was trying to say and do just the right thing. How I wished my dad was like Mr. Londeree!

That evening, when Mr. Londeree sat down beside me and asked how I was feeling, I snuggled up close to him and told him I wanted to be his little girl. He uttered a forced little laugh and started to pull away, but I wrapped my arms around his neck and kissed him firmly on the lips. I thought that would make him like me, but he just stood up abruptly and said, "No, Hallie, don't do that."

"Are you mad at me?" I asked.

"No, Hallie, it's just that—" He shook his head, flustered.

"Don't you like me?" I persisted.

"Yes, of course. You're very special to me, Hallie, but, well, there are proper ways for parents and children to touch and kiss one another. A little kiss on the cheek is enough to show me you care."

Later, when I pretended to be asleep on the sofa, I overheard Mr. and Mrs. Londeree talking in the other room. "She was making a pass at you tonight, Kevin," said Mrs. Londeree, sounding upset.

"You're making too much of it, Trish. She's just a child."

"No, she's not, Kevin. She's been taught all the wrong things about love. Now Hallie needs to learn healthy, positive ways of showing affection. She thinks everything has to be sexual."

"That's all she's ever known. How do we teach her differently?"

"By example, I suppose. And by teaching her self-control and how to set appropriate limits."

"That's a tall order," said Mr. Londeree.

"I know." Mrs. Londeree's voice turned sad. "So many abused kids think they will never have any sense of power or control except through sex, or any closeness with others except through sex. I hope we can show Hallie that that's not true."

I wasn't sure just what the Londerees' private conversation meant, but by bedtime I realized my special privileges were over. Mr. Londeree suggested I try walking upstairs on my crutches. I felt hurt. Maybe he didn't like me anymore. I put a little weight on my foot and groaned loudly. "It still hurts too much. Won't you please carry me?"

"The doctor wants you to use your crutches, Hallie."

"You carried me in the mountains," I argued.

"You didn't have any crutches in the mountains."

Robin joined us then and said, "I'll help you with Hallie, Dad." Together they helped me upstairs and over to my bed. "There you are," said Mr. Londeree. "Good night, Hallie. Sleep well."

"Will you tuck me in, please?" I asked softly. "And sit by my bed until I fall asleep?"

Mr. Londeree smiled and gently tousled my hair. "I think it'll be better if Mrs. Londeree tucks you in, Hallie. I'll call her."

I felt a stab of disappointment, but I rolled over and hugged my pillow tight. When Mrs. Londeree came in a minute later, I pretended I was already asleep.

The next day I returned to school, limping awkwardly and walking with my dumb crutches. I felt mortified, like everybody was looking at me and laughing and saying things behind my back.

At least I was able to leave school early. I had my first appointment that afternoon with the psychologist, Mrs. Flynn. Mrs. Londeree drove me and sat in the waiting room while I was ushered into Mrs. Flynn's private office. At least it was nice and plush with comfortable sofas and chairs, and Mrs. Flynn was young and attractive, not some ugly old bat. If I had to see a shrink, I was glad it was someone who looked and talked like Mrs. Flynn.

She was real casual and up-front. "I usually offer my clients coffee, Hallie," she said, "but I bet you'd rather have a Coke."

"No, thanks."

"Well, if your throat gets too dry from talking, you let me know, OK?"

"It won't," I mumbled. "I don't have anything to say."

Mrs. Flynn just smiled and asked me to sit down in a chair across from her desk. I sighed with relief, because in the movies the shrink always makes people lie down on a couch. I didn't want any of that. I sat down on the edge of the chair and twiddled my thumbs and tapped my toes. My heart was hammering. I wanted to get this over fast and get going.

But Mrs. Flynn just sat there, jotting something down on the papers on her desk, like she didn't even know I was there.

Finally I couldn't stand it any longer. I blurted, "How come I'm here? How come you aren't seeing my dad? He's the sicko."

Mrs. Flynn gave me a long, serious look. "That's very perceptive of you, Hallie," she said, sounding calm but firm. "What happened to you is entirely your father's responsibility. He does need help. I hope the court will see that he gets that help."

"They should put him away for a hundred years," I muttered.

"Is that what you want, Hallie—your father in prison?"

"No—yes—I don't know. Mom would kill me if they sent Dad to jail."

"Do you think she's angry with you over what happened?"

"I know she is. She hates me. She says I broke up our family."

Mrs. Flynn doodled something on her paper, then asked, "Is that how you feel, Hallie?"

I sat back in my chair and swung my good leg carelessly. "I don't know. Maybe I don't feel anything. Maybe I think this crummy meeting is a big waste of time."

"Is there anything at all you'd like to talk about, Hallie?"

"No."

Mrs. Flynn was silent for a minute. Then she smiled and asked, "How is your stay going with the Londerees?"

"OK, I guess."

"No problems?"

"No."

"And school? Has it been hard switching schools so early in the term?"

"It's a drag, but I'll manage. I liked Lincoln better."

"Are you saying you'd rather be living at home?"

"I didn't say that. Besides, they wouldn't let me now, not after I wrecked everything for them."

"Them?"

"Mom and Dad."

"Do you worry about how they feel toward you now?"

"No. It's no big deal."

"What about the way you feel toward them?"

"What do you mean?"

"I mean, you've hinted at their feelings toward you, but you haven't said how you feel about your parents."

"I don't get it. How am I supposed to feel?"

"That's what I'm asking you, Hallie."

I swung my bandaged leg and hit Mrs. Flynn's desk. My sore foot hurt. "I'm ticked off," I said.

"You're saying you're angry?"

"Wouldn't you be?"

"Tell me why, Hallie. Why are you angry at your parents?"

"I don't know."

"You don't know? Have you thought about it, Hallie?"

"I don't wanna think about it. I wanna forget the whole thing."

"Are you talking about your dad—how he hurt you?"

"Yeah, I wanna forget it, OK? Why does everybody make me talk about it—the police, the lawyers, and now you. Why can't I just forget? Forget, OK?"

Mrs. Flynn scribbled something else, off-handedly, like she was just marking time. "Can you forget, Hallie?"

I stared at the floor. "Can I go now? My ankle hurts."

Mrs. Flynn put her pencil down. "OK, Hallie. But we'll talk again soon. I'm here to help you. I hope you believe that."

I reached for my crutches, pulled myself up, and hobbled to the door. "Why should we talk again? I've said all I have to say."

As Mrs. Flynn opened the door, she smiled and said, "Humor me, OK, Hallie? I'll schedule you for this Friday. So long for now."

As I left Mrs. Flynn's office, I resolved to be more tight-lipped on Friday. Maybe I couldn't keep the cops from digging into the garbage about my dad, but that didn't mean I had to let some shrink mess with my head. So when Friday's appointment came, I sat down in the chair across from her desk and folded my arms across my chest, just daring Mrs. Flynn to pry any information out of me.

She chatted awhile about school and what my life was like at the Londerees' and what I wanted to be someday, all harmless stuff that didn't mean much. Finally, there was a minute of silence. Then she said, "You really don't want to talk about your father, do you?"

I felt a sudden spurt of resentment. "Why should I?"

"I just imagine you might like someone to talk to about your problems. I know I like having someone to talk to sometimes."

I slouched down in my seat. "But you're not me! You're not in my place. Nobody else is."

"So you think I can't understand how you feel? Is that it?"

When I didn't answer, she said, "Do you know, Hallie, that I've counseled many girls who've been sexually abused? Each one felt like she was the only girl in the world who had experienced such a tragedy." Mrs. Flynn met my gaze with sympathy. "You're not alone, Hallie."

"I never knew anyone else like me," I muttered sullenly.

Mrs. Flynn sat back in her chair and tapped her pen lightly on the desk. "Hallie, the statistics are pretty grim—one girl in four molested, sexually abused, or raped by the time she's eighteen. They all feel the same terrible pain you feel."

I didn't reply. Was Mrs. Flynn snowing me? I couldn't imagine anyone else feeling the guilt and shame I felt.

"You know, Hallie," continued Mrs. Flynn, "we have group sessions where girls talk with one another about their feelings. Perhaps one of these days you might like to join such a group."

I sat up straight and clutched the chair arms. "No way! You think I'm gonna blab everything to a bunch of strangers?"

"Very well, Hallie. For now it'll just be the two of us."

I sat back, relaxing a little.

"Tell me about your folks. Your mother works, doesn't she?"

"Yeah. She has for most of my life, I guess. She says Dad doesn't make enough money when he goes out selling."

"Are you and your mom close, Hallie?"

I shrugged. "I don't see much of her."

"Does that bother you?"

"It used to when I was little."

"And now?"

"No big deal. Mom's a waitress. She works at night."

"Are you saying she wasn't around to read you bedtime stories or tuck you in or play games?"

"That's kiddie stuff."

"But your dad was there, wasn't he?"

"Yeah, I guess so. He felt bad about Mom being gone so much. She made him feel guilty about not earning enough money so she could stay home. Sometimes she would yell at him just like Grandma Shay always did. Then my dad would get real depressed."

"And you would try to comfort him?"

"Yeah, I tried." The memories started flashing back in my mind. "Dad always said I was the only one who could make him feel better."

"How did you make him feel better, Hallie?"

"I—don't remember."

"When you were a little girl, Hallie, how did it start—the bad times with your dad?"

I stared into space, remembering, seeing myself as this happy, bubbly little kid. "I—I would climb up on Dad's lap when he looked sad. I'd pat his face or give him a hug or kiss to cheer him up. I liked it when he held me in his arms and rocked me. I felt so safe. He said he loved me more than anyone else in the world."

"How did you feel about those times, Hallie?"

"I—I liked them." I blinked back sudden tears. "I liked being close to my dad. I wanted him to love me."

"How do you feel now when you talk about wanting to love your dad?"

I choked out the words. "I—I feel bad—dirty inside. I was a bad girl. I didn't mean it, Mrs. Flynn. Honest, I didn't. I just wanted my dad to hold me and love me."

Mrs. Flynn sat forward intently. "Listen, Hallie, this is very important. You weren't a bad girl. Every little girl wants her father to hold her and love her. But your father took advantage of your trust and your innocence to make you do things you didn't want to do. You had no choice, no control over your circumstances. Your dad was wrong, Hallie, not you. Can you understand that?"

I was sobbing now, trying to hold back the sobs, my chest heaving uncontrollably. "My dad said it was my fault," I cried. "He said I teased him; I asked for it! He said if I told, everyone would know what a bad girl I was." My words were coming in short, halting gasps. "And that's how I feel. That's how I feel every minute, every day! I feel like the worst scum in the whole wide world!"

12

After talking with Mrs. Flynn, I wasn't in any mood to attend the Sadie Hawkins party at church that evening. I'd be a fifth wheel, tagging along with Robin and Darin and Zena and her date. Like, I'd be a total misfit, you know?

I kept thinking that I'd rather be with Matt. But the Londerees acted like they just naturally expected me to go to the church party. Mrs. Londeree even had a costume ready for me—bib overalls, striped shirt, bandanna, and a straw hat. I absolutely refused the straw hat, but Zena said she'd wear it. It would give a new country look to her spiked hair.

I met Robin's handsome hunk, Darin Chadbourne, that evening. He was tall and dark with a mass of coal-black hair and terrific smoky gray eyes. I saw right away that he had the same kind of movie-actor good looks my dad had. Like when he looked right at you, you felt all goose-bumpy and dry-mouthed, and if you tried to string a bunch of words together in a sensible sentence, you couldn't possibly do it.

When Robin introduced us, Darin smiled and said, "Glad to meet you, Hallie." His voice was low and serious, like he would never say anything without thinking it through carefully first. "We'd better get going," he told Robin. "It's a long drive to the Chandler farm, and we've still got to pick up Roger."

"Oh, my gorgeous Roger." Zena sighed dreamily. "The love of my life—if only I can convince him!"

"Well, Zena, you have a whole evening to try." Robin laughed.

"Half an evening if we don't leave now," warned Darin.

As we three girls piled into Darin's silver-blue Mustang and he tossed my crutches into the trunk, I tried to convince myself I had nothing to be nervous about. But the closer we got to the Chandler farm, the less persuasive my arguments sounded. While the two couples chatted happily, I sank more and more into my own dark little world of silence. I didn't want to see anybody; I didn't want to talk with anyone. I had no business trotting off to some party with a bunch of people I didn't even know. For the first time since coming to the Londerees' home, I wished I could flee back to my own house and hide. But no, never! Was I forgetting so easily, so quickly? That was enemy territory too. There was nowhere I could run to be safe and free.

A few minutes later, when we approached the huge, old, brightly decorated barn, I knew my worst fears would be realized. I would be a spectacle in this place, an oddball, an object of dark curiosity. I could imagine the questions in everyone's mind: *Who is this funny little stranger on crutches, with the frightened eyes and ordinary face? Surely she's not one of us. What is she doing here?*

I followed Robin and Darin inside the barn, but they quickly melted into the crowd. I gazed in pure panic at the dozens of kids milling around in their country-western threads, all laughing and shouting and talking at once. Streamers and paper lanterns hung everywhere, and the aromas of popcorn and caramel apples mingled with the earthy barn smells.

I made my way awkwardly over to the refreshment table and grabbed a paper cup of hot cider, then inched over to one corner and leaned against the rough-hewn barn wall. I still felt like everyone was staring at me and my crutches, giving me dirty looks, like I had green hair or B.0. or zits all over my face. I felt ugly, ugly, ugly. I started thinking real crazy things, like, *maybe they know about what I did with my father.* Maybe they're wondering, *What's that scum, that untouchable, doing here at a nice Christian party?*

For a half hour I just stood there standing stiff as a ruler, listening to the lively fiddle music and rollicking laughter, afraid to look anybody in the eye. Then, when I went back for more cider, a gawky, skinny boy bumped into me accidentally and said, "Excuse me." I just glared at him like he'd slugged me or something.

A couple of girls I'd met in Sunday school went by and said hi, and I said hi back, but the word came out so low, I know they didn't hear me. Finally, after what seemed forever, Robin and Darin came strolling through the crowd toward me, all smiling and bubbly like they were having the best time ever. "Hey, Hallie, we wondered where you disappeared to," said Robin. "Come join in the games. They're outta sight!"

"No, I can't with these crutches," I protested. "Besides, I don't like dumb games."

But then Darin got in the act and slung his arm around my shoulder in a comradely sort of way. For an instant I drew back sharply, like I'd been burned or something, but then it felt kind of nice so I left his arm there and even inched a little closer to him.

"You gotta come play 'Needle in the Haystack,' Hallie," he said in that smooth, slow voice of his. "They planted two ten dollar bills in that pile of straw over there, and everyone's gonna be looking for them. Come on. I bet you could use ten bucks, right?"

I was weakening fast, and Darin knew it. "Look, Robin," he said, "Hallie wants to play. I can see the dollar signs in her eyes."

"You're right," Robin teased. "The whites of her eyes are turning positively green."

"OK, all right," I said, relenting. "I'll play."

Robin and Darin promptly marched me over to this colossal haystack, and the next thing I knew, someone was shouting, "Get ready, get set, go!" Instantly everyone was scrambling and diving headlong into that huge mountain of straw. Hay was flying everywhere, and the fresh alfalfa smell filled the whole barn.

As I threw my crutches aside and dove into the haystack, I didn't care about finding the money. I was more interested in grabbing handfuls of straw and stuffing them down the back of Darin's shirt. He retaliated by stuffing straw down my neck. "Hey, the little hayseed's turning foolhardy!" he declared. "Here's a taste of your own medicine, rube!"

Within minutes our good-natured roughhousing escalated to all-out war, the two of us smushing hay in each other's face and rolling on the ground in blind, wild combat.

"Hallie, stop!" cried Robin. "Darin, be careful of Hallie's leg! Hallie, your ankle!"

I felt totally detached from Robin's cries. I was caught up instead in a strange, obsessive frenzy that both exhilarated and terrified me. I just kept swinging and pounding and hitting Darin. I couldn't stop.

"Hey, Hallie, cut it out!" Darin sputtered breathlessly as I hammered his chest with my fists. Then, in one swift move he gripped my arms and pushed me off him.

I fell sprawling back on the straw-matted ground, momentarily dazed and exhausted. My chest heaved as I gasped hungrily for air. I looked around, aware suddenly that everyone had stopped searching the haystack and was staring down at me. "What happened?" someone asked.

"They were fighting," said someone else. "Or maybe they were just playing around."

"If that was play, it looked pretty fierce to me," mused a chunky girl standing beside Robin.

I shook my head, baffled, trying to throw off my confusion. I didn't know what had happened any more than they did. It was crazy. Was I beating on Darin to hurt him, or to get him to like me, or was I just pounding on him because it felt good?

Darin stood up awkwardly and brushed bits of straw from his Levi's. He was laughing huskily like it was all a big joke. "It's cool, guys. Hallie and I were just having a little fun." He looked around at everyone and grinned. "Come on, laugh! Get with it! I learned my lesson good. This little girl's a regular wildcat. A real little spitfire."

He ambled over to me, helped me up and handed me my crutches. Pulling a wisp of straw from my tousled hair, he whispered confidentially, "You know, Hallie, with all that pent-up hostility, you should join the school wrestling team."

By now all the kids were turning their attention back to the haystack. Darin pivoted breezily and sauntered off with Robin. I heard him tell her under his breath, "She may be your sweet little foster sister, Robin, but I thought for sure she was going to kill me."

13

Would you believe?—Saturday was my birthday. My life was so different these days that I'd hardly had time to think about it. And with the humiliation of Friday night's Sadie Hawkins party still fresh in my mind—my trashing Robin's precious Darin—I awoke on Saturday feeling my usual nameless guilt and thinking it was just another ordinary day.

Then, after I'd dressed in my Mickey Mouse shirt and comfy sweats and started downstairs, I smelled a cake baking. Yummy chocolate. And I remembered. My birthday. Incredible. I was fourteen today. That should have meant something special. I should have felt young and happy and tingly alive, my life bursting with all sorts of possibilities. Instead I felt like I was hanging in limbo, not a kid, not an adult. I didn't fit in anywhere. I felt like fourteen going on forty.

At breakfast, Mrs. Londeree said, "Hallie, your mother has asked to see you today, but it's up to you."

"You mean, she wants to come here?"

"Yes. Right after dinner, if you agree."

"Yeah, sure. I'd like that," I said, trying not to let my excitement show. Mom had remembered my birthday after all!

The rest of the day was brighter now that I knew I'd see Mom again. I missed her. Ever since the day she'd walked out on me at the Beatrice Crown Home, I'd felt a terrible knot of disappointment in my stomach. I hated having Mom mad at me. But now, since she was coming to visit, maybe that meant she liked me after all.

I was glad that Mrs. Londeree fixed an early dinner. She served sizzling charbroiled steak, baked potatoes, and a tossed salad. Then came the cake—chocolate fudge with mounds of white frosting and fourteen blazing candles. Robin and her parents sang "Happy Birthday" to me, then I made a wish—*Let my parents and me be a family again!*—and blew out the candles. Good grief, all but one! It figured. My wishes never came true anyway.

After we'd devoured the cake and ice cream, Robin and Mrs. Londeree handed me a stack of presents wrapped in ribbons and glittering foil. Suddenly it felt like the best of every holiday I'd ever known. I tore open the packages and gazed with pleasure at the new school dress and the comb and brush set. And there was a makeup kit and shampoo and costume jewelry.

I was just unwrapping the last gift when Mom arrived carrying packages of her own. She looked tense and a little frazzled. Her hair was windblown, and her apple-red lipstick was smeared on her upper lip. Mrs. Londeree showed us into the family room where Mom and I could have some time alone together. I could see that Mom was relieved that she wouldn't have to make small talk with my foster family. She sat down on the sofa and handed me the gifts—one large one and one small one.

While I opened the large one, Mom said, "I'm sorry about your sprained ankle. Is it very painful?"

"Not anymore," I answered. "I hardly need the crutches now."

"Well, that's good." She was silent for a minute, then asked, "So how are the Londerees treating you, Hallie?"

"Real nice. They make me feel welcome. I think they like me."

"Well, sure, Hallie. Who wouldn't?" She hesitated. "Don't you miss your family?"

I stared at the floor. "Yes, but—"

"We miss you too, Hallie. Your dad and I just rattle around in that house without you." She reached over and pulled off a strip of wrapping paper on the large gift. "I think you'll like this, Hallie."

I opened the box and took out a large photo album. It was brimming over with old pictures of our family from the time I was born.

"I thought you might like something to remember us by, honey."

"Thanks, Mom," I murmured. I set it aside and picked up the small gift.

"That's from your dad. He picked it out himself."

I removed the foil wrap, then carefully opened a little velvet jewelry box. Inside was a sparkling gold locket. "Oh, Mom, it's gorgeous!" I flipped it open and for an instant drew back in revulsion. It was a picture of my dad. He was smiling like nothing in the world could be wrong. I let it fall on the floor by my feet.

Mom pretended not to notice. She handed me a sealed envelope and said, "This is from your dad too, but don't read it until after I go." She took a hankie from her pocket and touched it daintily to her nose. "Your father loves you very much, Hallie, whether you choose to believe it or not."

"If Dad really loved me, he wouldn't have hurt me. Besides, why should I believe either one of you?" I countered. "You don't believe anything *I* say."

Mom sat forward. "How can I believe you when you've made me choose between you and your father, Hallie? Your dad wouldn't lie to me, I know that." She sighed heavily. "Your father's a broken man, Hallie. He was fired from his job, you know. His boss found out about the arrest."

"I'm sorry," I murmured.

Mom gave me a sudden, shrewd look. "If you would just admit that you lied, Hallie, I'm sure your dad could get his job back."

"I didn't lie."

"Your dad and I wouldn't even punish you, Hallie. We'd figure you'd learned your lesson."

"Don't you hear me? I wasn't lying, Mom."

"We could all be a family again, Hallie, just like before," Mom pleaded, her eyes red-rimmed with an anguish I'd never seen before. "It's not too late—"

I stood up, clenching my fists until my whole body began to shake. "I can't go back, Mom! I can't, I can't, I can't!"

Mom was motionless a moment, as if drawing her grief back inside herself. Then she stood up in a huff and said, "I'll never understand you, Hallie, never! How you can be so stubborn and cruel!"

"Please, Mom, try, try to understand," I begged. "I have a chance now. I feel like I could be free—free like a—a butterfly."

Mom stiffened with disdain. "That's nonsense, Hallie!"

"But, Mom, if I go home now, it'll be like crawling back into a dirty little cocoon. I'll be all trapped and helpless and suffocating again. I'll shrivel up and die, Mom. Don't you see? I'll die!"

Mom waved her hand breezily, dismissing me. "Oh, Hallie, you're always so dramatic about everything. You're young and healthy. You're a long way from dying."

I went to Mom and forced myself to meet her gaze. My voice came out quivery and uneven. "I die a little inside every time Dad touches me, Mom. I'd rather die all at once than go back and die inch by inch with him."

Mom's face reddened with fury. "I simply can't reason with you, can I, Hallie?" She picked up her purse and squared her shoulders. "I came here today to ask you not to testify at the preliminary hearing next Monday—"

"The hearing? It's on Monday?"

"Yes. Didn't you know?"

"Maybe—I don't know—I forgot."

"Well, the prosecution won't have a case if you don't testify, Hallie. You've punished your dad enough. Now it's time to call off this insanity and come home where you belong."

I walked over to the window and stared outside. A headache was starting somewhere at the back of my head, matching my pulse beat for beat. "Tell Dad I said thanks for the presents, Mom."

We stared at each other for a long, silent moment. Then a fire of animosity glinted in Mom's eyes. "I bet you feel real smug, don't you, daughter, making everyone think your dad prefers you to me? Well, it won't work. Our lawyer will blow you away on the witness stand. If it's the last thing he does, he'll make you confess these hellish lies of yours!"

With that, Mom stormed out. I didn't even try to stop her. I just collapsed back on the sofa and stared into space. I kept thinking, *Why do the people I love most make me feel the worst?* It wasn't supposed to be this way, was it? Was it like this for other kids?

Then, with my hands still trembling, I tore open the envelope from my dad. It was a letter, handwritten in Dad's familiar scrawl. It said:

Dear Hallie:

   I just had to write you on your special day. It's hard to believe my little girl is growing up, but no matter how old you are you'll still be my little girl. I just wanted you to know I don't hold anything against you for what you've done. I forgive you for all the trouble you've caused, and no matter what they do to me, I won't be mad at you. Your old man just wants his little girl home with him again so we can be the happy family we were before. We don't need outsiders prying into our family business, honey. We can handle whatever problems we have on our own. Please give me another chance to prove how important you are to me, sweetheart. I hope you like the locket. Happy Birthday.

                              Your loving Dad

   I sat forward on the sofa and let the letter fall from my hands. Something awful was happening in my head, a geyser of emotions erupting inside me, spewing up a venomous, dark rage. A scream rose from my throat and shattered the silence. I couldn't stop it; the terrible, bone-chilling sound just kept coming from inside me.

   I was aware suddenly of the Londerees and Robin rushing into the room, surrounding me, Mrs. Londeree trying to reach out to me, me pushing her away, the scream still emerging from my lips in a piercing, agonized shriek.

"Call Mrs. Flynn," cried Mrs. Londeree.

Mr. Londeree ran to the phone. Robin tried to touch my shoulder, my arm, but I pushed her away. I grabbed up my locket and threw it against the wall, then raised the photo album over my head and slammed it to the floor. Pictures flew out on the rug, and I crushed them into the carpet with my crutch.

"I can't reach Mrs. Flynn on Saturday," said Mr. Londeree. "I just got her answering service."

"She's so angry, it scares me," cried Mrs. Londeree.

The blinding fury was ebbing a little. I could feel the mushrooming hatred winding back down in on itself. It was all squeezing back into my chest, bringing back the tight, aching sensation I lived with all the time. I started to cry.

Robin put her arms around me. I didn't push her away this time.

"What is it, Hallie?" she asked softly. "Are your parents mad at you? Is that it?"

"No—no." I wept. "They're killing me with their love!"

Robin looked up blankly at her folks and asked, "How can we help her? What do we do?"

Mrs. Londeree came over and wiped a tear from my cheek. "How can we help you, Hallie?"

I was still shaking from head to toe. "I don't know what to do with all the anger. I'm so, so furious."

"There's nothing wrong with being angry, Hallie," said Mr. Londeree. "It's a feeling, and feelings aren't good or bad. They're just there. It's not just how you feel, Hallie; it's what you do with the feeling that counts."

"In fact, feelings are very important, Hallie," said Mrs. Londeree. "Feelings are the most beautiful gift you can give another human being."

I looked up pleadingly. "But how can I stop feeling so mad inside?"

"Well, you can't tear up the house, that's for sure," she said kindly. "But you could do what I used to tell Robin when she was angry and stomping around."

I looked at Robin. "What's that?"

Robin chuckled self-consciously. "I used to take a foam-rubber bat and go down in the basement and hit things with it. It sounds really stupid, but—"

"Well," said Mr. Londeree, "when I feel angry or frustrated, I jog a few miles or go downstairs and do a few rounds with my punching bag. It releases my anger in a nondestructive way."

"Come on, Hallie," said Robin. "I know just where that bat is."

I followed her down to the basement thinking the whole thing sounded a little crazy. But once I was alone and had that big, orange, foam-rubber bat in my hands, it felt good, like I really did have some power, some control over what I was doing. I started by giving the stair steps a few whacks; then I hit some old storage barrels. Pretty soon I was battering the concrete walls for all I was worth. And all the while I was shouting at my mom and dad, telling them how I felt about things, pouring all the hurt and venom out to four walls that couldn't even respond. "How can you say you love me, Dad, when you keep hurting me?" I screamed. "Why can't you say you're sorry for what you've done? Why does it all have to be my fault? Why do I have to carry all the shame alone? And you, Mom, why didn't you take care of me so Dad wouldn't hurt me? Why can't you both see that you're killing me?"

I must have stayed down in the basement for over an hour, striking everything in sight with that big rubber bat. But when I finally climbed the stairs, panting and exhausted, I knew I'd never felt better in my life. I stumbled up to my room and collapsed on my bed, trying to catch my breath.

After a while, Robin knocked at my door, then came in and sat at the foot of my bed. "Do you feel like some company?" she asked.

"I—I guess so."

"I just wanted to tell you something I learned awhile back."

"Yeah? What?"

"It's just that after you get the anger out of your body, you still need to get it out of your mind."

"How do you do that?"

"Well, I do it by telling someone."

"Who?"

"Jesus."

"Like in church, you mean?"

"Well, maybe, but mostly right here at home."

"I don't get it. You mean praying?"

"Yes. Talking to God when I'm alone in my room or when I'm out walking in the woods, wherever."

I stared down at my hands, at the dirt under the half moon of my fingernail. "I don't know anything about God."

Robin moved over closer to me. "Well, He wants to be your friend, Hallie."

I dug at my nail, loosening the dirt. "No, He doesn't."

"Yes, Hallie. He loves you. That's why He sent His Son to die for you."

I stood up abruptly. "Look, Robin, I didn't ask anybody to die for me." I walked over to the window and looked outside. The leaves were already turning orange and golden yellow. In a small voice, I told Robin, "Besides, I'm nobody. Who would die for me?"

"Jesus."

"Jesus is a fairy story they tell kids in church."

"No, Hallie. He's real."

I turned back to Robin. "How do you know?"

"Because I know Him. He's living in my heart right now."

"Oh, come on. How can He do that?"

"I don't know, Hallie. It's a miracle."

"I don't believe in miracles."

"But it's true, Hallie. When I was twelve, I asked Jesus to be my Savior. His Holy Spirit came into my heart and made me clean and new." Robin came over beside me, her face bright with excitement. "And now, Hallie, Jesus is always there for me to share with and tell my problems to. He makes me feel happy and peaceful inside. He could help you too, Hallie."

I shook my head. "You don't know me, Robin. I'm not like you. I'm not the religious type."

"I'm not just talking about being religious, Hallie. I'm talking about having a relationship with a real Person. Jesus."

I laughed huskily. "I'm not exactly the type God would want on His side, Robin. I might give Him a bad reputation." My voice turned somber. "Besides, even God couldn't help me."

Robin reached out and put her hand on my arm. Gently she asked, "How do you know, Hallie, unless you give Him a chance?"

I pulled away and turned back to the window and gazed again at the crisp autumn leaves blowing in the October wind. Sadly I reflected, *How can I make Robin understand? If God really knew me, He wouldn't even like me. He'd never want to live in my heart.*

14

On Sunday morning I went with Robin to her Sunday school class, but after a few minutes I leaned over and whispered, "I gotta go to the rest room." I slipped out before she could reply. I just couldn't hack it with all those goody-goodies and their talk about sex being created by God and all. Man, what I knew about sex was straight from hell.

On my way down the hall I stopped by the little kids' class again. Just like last week, I stood outside their door and listened to them sing. How I longed to be one of them, with their innocent, clean-scrubbed faces and trusting eyes. No one had scribbled obscenities over their souls; they were still pure, untouched.

I swallowed as the children sang "Jesus Loves Me," but it was the words of another song that caught my attention like a thunderclap:

> What can wash away my sin?
> Nothing but the blood of Jesus;
> What can make me whole again?
> Nothing but the blood of Jesus.

The song baffled me. Intrigued me. Why would innocent little kids sing about sin and blood? What did they know about such things? What did the words really mean? Was it possible to wash away sins, like taking a shower or something? But how? The song said Jesus' blood. But how could Jesus' blood make someone whole again—*someone broken like me?*

My heart was pounding as I walked on down to the end of the hall where a painting of Jesus hung. I stared up at the picture, trying to figure it out. "Are the kids right, Jesus?" I asked. "Do You love me?" His strong face and warm, gentle eyes seemed real. But His long hair and beard reminded me of pictures I'd seen of hippies from the sixties. Yet Jesus didn't look like the hippie type; He didn't look like any type I'd ever known. He looked like someone I *wished* I knew. I whispered again, "Well, do you love me, Jesus?"

I was almost trembling. Then a dark thought struck me: *He's a man. You can't trust any man. They pretend to love you just so they can hurt you!* With a shiver of dread, I turned abruptly and rounded the corner to the ladies' room. I stayed there, idly leaning against the sink until Sunday school was over.

By Monday morning a brand new fear had crowded out my questions about Jesus. Today was the preliminary hearing for my dad. I would have to tell the judge—a complete stranger!—all that my dad and I had done. Then he would know what a terrible person I was. Why, oh, why couldn't I just die and be born again as one of those sweet little kids in Sunday school? But I already knew the answer. There was nothing on earth that could patch up Hallie Shay and make her a brand-new, innocent baby.

Mrs. Londeree drove me downtown to the courthouse. But she had to stay in the victim witness room. My fingers felt like icicles, and my stomach hurt like mad as I was ushered into the courtroom. I couldn't remember ever feeling so scared, except maybe some of those nights with my dad.

My attorney, Mr. Stone, was already there, shuffling some papers and looking very businesslike. When he saw me, he beckoned for me to sit down beside him. I dutifully took my seat. Then from the corner of my eye I spotted Mom and Dad entering from another door. They were with a man I didn't know. Dad's attorney, I figured. They sat down without looking my way.

Mr. Stone leaned over and whispered, "Remember, Hallie, this hearing will determine whether there's sufficient evidence to bring your father's case before a jury. So be very exact with your answers."

"I'll try," I murmured, swallowing over the lump in my throat. A sober-faced judge in a long, black robe came in and sat down behind his enormous desk. He looked so powerful, I couldn't imagine him ever being just an ordinary person in an old shirt and Levi's.

He was barely settled when I was called as the first witness. I walked up in a daze and sat down in the chair by the judge's desk. As I was sworn in, my eyes kept darting to my dad's face.

It was all I could do to concentrate on my attorney's strange questions about who I was and who my parents were. He nodded toward my dad. "Hallie, let me direct your attention to the man, Howard Vernon Shay, sitting at the defense table. Is he related to you?"

I gave Mr. Stone a puzzled look. "Sure. He's my dad."

Immediately Dad's attorney shouted, "Objection! That's hearsay."

For several minutes the two attorneys argued back and forth about whether I was actually my father's child. I just sat and stared at them in bewilderment. Finally I heard my dad tell his attorney, "Drop it, will you? She's my kid."

Everything went downhill from there—four hours of embarrassing, humiliating questions. The two attorneys asked me the same thing over and over until I thought I would scream.

Dad's defense attorney was a real bear. He did all he could to trip me up. He'd say, "Hallie, can you tell me a specific day when a sexual encounter occurred between you and the defendant?"

I'd say, "Yes, sir. The last night I was home before I went to the police."

"What day was that, Hallie?"

"Friday."

"Which month, and what day of the month, Hallie?"

"It was about two weeks ago."

"The specific date, Hallie."

"September—I don't remember if it was the twenty-eighth or twenty-ninth."

"We need the exact date, Hallie."

"Friday. Was that the twenty-eighth?"

My attorney spoke up and said, "Will the court please record that the Friday in question was the twenty-ninth."

"Objection," said Dad's attorney. "Let the witness speak for herself."

"She did speak," replied Mr. Stone. "She just doesn't have a calendar to check, and I do. I don't think there's any question about which Friday night she means. She filed a complaint with the police on Saturday, September thirtieth."

Dad's attorney grudgingly went on. "All right, Hallie, will you please recount the events of Friday, September twenty-ninth?"

"I already did."

"Would you please begin again with what you say happened after your father entered your bedroom on the night of September twenty-ninth?"

"I told you before."

"Would you please recount, step by step, the events of that evening, in detail this time?"

I tried to force out the words, but they stuck in my throat. I looked over at Dad. His face was white and drained. I tried again to speak. "Well, uh—my dad—he came into my room and asked if I was awake. But I pretended like I was asleep. Then my dad—he—he—"

"Go on, Hallie," the attorney prompted.

"Well, my dad, he—he started touching me—"

131

"Please be more specific, Hallie."

"You know, fondling . . ."

"Where, Hallie?"

I stared in desperation at my dad. I could see his hands gripping the chair arm. His face looked like it was about to shatter. I sat forward and clenched my fists and screamed, "Please, Dad, please make them stop. Don't make me say it! You tell them—you tell them what you did to me!"

My dad put his head in his hands and began to sob.

The judge pounded his gavel on the desk and shouted, "Order, order, please!"

I started crying too. I couldn't stop. Finally the judge said, "Let's call a recess. We'll adjourn for a half hour."

During the break I went to the bathroom and washed my face and kept the wet paper towel on my forehead for a few minutes. My head hurt so bad it felt like it would explode. I kept wondering if there was some way I could sneak away and go see Matt, but as soon as I left the rest room, Mr. Stone was waiting for me. He handed me a 7-Up and told me I was doing very well. We walked back down the hall to the victim witness room. Inside, I was surprised—and pleased—to see Mrs. Wilcox, my case worker, sitting beside Mrs. Londeree.

Mrs. Wilcox got right up and came over to me. "Hello, Hallie," she said, smiling. "I'm sorry I couldn't get here before you testified. I wanted you to know I'm rooting for you."

"I still have to go back in," I told her as we sat down.

"I know, Hallie."

"Can you come in with me?"

"No, Hallie, I can't. It's against the rules."

"Whose rules?"

"Oh, I don't know. The judicial system's, I suppose. I'm sorry."

"When will it be over?" I asked plaintively.

"I don't know, Hallie."

"Today?"

"Maybe, maybe not. We'll have to wait and see."

"Do I have to tell the judge all the gross stuff my dad did?"

"I'm afraid so, Hallie. I know how hard it is for you."

"How do you know?" I snapped. "You don't have to do it."

"No, Hallie, but I do know it's a very painful thing to do. But this is the only way we can try to make things right in your family."

"Ha!" I scoffed. "Now that I've ratted on my dad, we won't ever be a family again. My parents hate me. They think I'm a traitor."

"Is that how you feel, Hallie?"

"Sometimes. I don't know. Everything's all mixed up inside. Sometimes I hate my dad so much I wanna kill him." I drew in a deep breath. "Other times I'm scared to death he won't love me anymore."

"Believe it or not, those are normal feelings, Hallie."

I looked up at Mrs. Wilcox. "Is it normal to feel so dirty inside, like something crawling under a rock? That's how Dad's attorney makes me feel, like he's getting all charged over this whole gaggy mess."

Mrs. Wilcox shook her head somberly. "To tell you the truth, Hallie, court hearings like this turn my stomach too. The judicial system is far from perfect. But, for now, this is all we've got. So if you can, just make yourself go out there and lay it all on the line. And keep in mind that in the long run you'll be helping your dad, your mom, and yourself."

"That's what I don't get. How will my testimony help anyone?"

Mrs. Wilcox cleared her throat and said, "Hallie, your family had a cancer in it, and you're the only one who was brave enough to do something about it. Maybe because of you your father, and your mother too, will get the help they need to make their lives healthy again. Whether they seek help or not, Hallie, you can survive because you've begun to cut out the cancer. You have the freedom now to be whole and healthy. Don't you see, Hallie? You have the choice to make your life whatever you want."

Mrs. Londeree leaned over and smiled at me. "I agree with Mrs. Wilcox, Hallie. And I want you to know there are many of us who will do everything we can to help you and stand by you."

"Who?" I murmured, staring down at my hands.

"Well, my family, of course, and Mrs. Wilcox, and Mrs. Flynn, your psychologist, and Mr. Stone—and your teachers—"

Before Mrs. Londeree could finish, the door opened and a man poked his nose inside and said, "Miss Hallie Shay, we're ready for you in the courtroom."

Mrs. Wilcox reached over and squeezed my hand. "Good luck, Hallie. Just give it your best."

Mrs. Londeree patted my arm and said, "I'll be whispering a prayer for you, Hallie."

"Yeah, thanks," I said, standing up and squaring my shoulders. "I'll need it."

15

The next morning I was back at Tisdale High like nothing had ever happened. Actually, it was a relief to be back in school after yesterday's nightmare at the courthouse. And the interrogation wasn't over yet. The preliminary hearing was scheduled to pick up again on Thursday. I'm sure I dreaded it more than my dad did. I knew he would go on maintaining his innocence, no matter what I said. I hated him for that, almost more than I hated him for all the years of abuse. Before, the humiliation had been private; now I was being forced to spill my guts to the whole world. I wondered, *What kind of father would dump on his own kid that way?*

At noon I joined Robin and Zena in the cafeteria for lunch, but I kept my mouth shut and just concentrated on my macaroni and cheese. Zena didn't know about the court hearing. No one outside Robin's family knew, and I wanted to keep it that way.

I didn't have to worry about keeping up my end of the conversation because Zena was doing great all by herself. "Listen, Robin," she bubbled, "like, you know, I got this new pop-art miniskirt, and it's super awesome. It's electric blue, you know? And would you believe? My mom sees it and says, 'Oh, you bought a little doggie outfit for Fritzy?' And I say, 'Fer sure, Mom! Be real! That's my new miniskirt.' And my mom freaks out and starts laying all this heavy stuff on me about being a proper young lady and all. Then she sees the jazzy lace tights I bought, and like she accuses me of being some femme fatale. I mean, like, I was so bummed at my mom!"

"Zena, your heavenly hash—uh, goulash—is getting cold," Robin said.

Zena snorted in disgust. "Man, like, that slop needs a proper burial! Besides, I gotta lose five pounds so I can get into my new Capri pants. I mean, they are totally rad. They're Aztec print, and they just match Roger's new retro-fifties surf shorts. I mean, they are outta sight!"

Just when I figured I couldn't tolerate another cutesy comment from Zena, some guy I'd never seen before comes over to the table and nudges me. "Hey, Hallie—you Hallie Shay?"

"Yeah. Who wants to know?"

"My buddy and I got a bet on. He says your dad's some fancy ambassador. That right?"

My pulse started racing. "Well, uh, yeah, sure, he—he's an ambassador."

"Yeah, that a fact? Is his name Howard Vernon Shay?"

"Yes, but how did you know—?"

With a triumphant sneer, the boy waved a newspaper clipping in my face. "This article here talks about a preliminary hearing for a man by that name," he drawled smugly. "Looks like he's accused of sexually abusing his teenage daughter. It don't give her name, of course, but looks like we all know who that is, don't we!"

For an instant I couldn't breathe. I stared at the boy. He stared back. I thought, *Why would a stranger want to hurt me? Why is he doing this?*

"So looks like I win the bet, right?" said the boy. "Your old man's no more an ambassador than mine is. Looks more like he's some kind of pervert—"

I sprang from my chair and shoved the boy with all my might. He sprawled backward in a surprised heap. "Hey, you, I'll get even," he sputtered.

I was already running out of the cafeteria, pushing my way through the crowd, fighting back hot, angry tears. I made my way blindly to the girls' gym, darted into the locker room, and sat down on a bench and sobbed.

Finally the door opened, and Robin and Zena came in. Robin came over and sat beside me and slipped her arm around my shoulder. "It's OK, Hallie," she soothed. "Don't pay any attention to a geek like that. He's trash."

"If I ever catch him alone, he's dead," I bawled.

Zena sat down on the other side of me. "Listen, Hallie, like, I don't know what to say, but

Robin just told me what all's going down on you, and I mean, like, it's really a bummer. Here I thought I had problems—!"

I kept right on blubbering. "I—I didn't want anyone to know!"

"Sure, I understand. You must feel like the whole crazy world's dumping on you. But you know what I think, Hallie?"

I didn't answer. I knew Zena would tell me anyway.

"I think you're a survivor, Hallie. You cut out on a real bad scene. Now you don't have to take any guff from your old man anymore. You can call the shots in your life. I think that's cool."

"Zena's right," said Robin. "You've got a whole new life ahead of you, Hallie. Don't feel guilty about what your dad did. Forget him. You'll feel better when you put it all behind you."

I shook my head. "How do either of you know how I feel? You don't know me. I don't even know how I feel. How can I know when nothing in my life makes any sense?"

Zena gazed helplessly at Robin. "Go on, Robin. Say something. You're the one with all the answers from the Bible."

Robin smiled gently. "Hallie, you're right. I don't really know how you feel. I've never been hurt like you have. I don't have all the answers, but I do have Jesus. He's my best Friend. He's the One with the answers."

"Yeah, sure," I mumbled, wiping my eyes. I stood up and smoothed my shirt over my jeans. "We better go, or we'll be late to fifth period."

As it turned out, I was ten minutes early to my fifth period class. I stood outside the door, waiting for fourth period to clear out. Suddenly someone jostled me, and I nearly dropped my books. I looked around and recognized the dude from the cafeteria. He was with three other guys. They were all looking at me and laughing. Then one of the geeks chanted mockingly, "Hallie Shay, Hallie Shay. How her daddy likes to play!"

I whirled around and slammed my algebra book into his stomach. He let out a stunned gasp of air and doubled over. Swiftly his buddy sprang forward and gripped my wrist. "So, the girl likes to play too, huh? I bet with all your experience you really know the score!"

I pulled frantically, twisting and tugging to free myself, but the jerk just laughed viciously and tightened his hold. Suddenly my algebra teacher came bounding into the hallway, shouting, "Students, stop! Now! Break it up!"

For the rest of the afternoon, all I could think of was that more people were discovering the secret I had guarded so fiercely since I was seven. During the preliminary hearing I'd learned an important word: *violation.* My dad had violated me physically. But lately I was learning there were different kinds of violation. They all hurt. They all made me feel ashamed.

I didn't wait to meet Robin and Zena after school. I wanted to walk home by myself. I had a lot of thinking to do. But minutes after I'd left the high school campus, a girl from my algebra class came running up to me. She was one of those bookworm types who always knows all the answers and gets an A on every test. She'd never spoken to me before, so I was surprised when she started walking along beside me, matching my stride.

"Hi, I'm Beverly," she said. "We have algebra together."

"Yeah, I know. I'm Hallie."

"I know," she said softly. We walked a few moments in silence. Then she started talking to me in a real low, confidential voice. "I know who you are. I read the paper. I suspected, but then when the boys teased you today—" She paused and looked at me. "I'm not trying to be cruel. Please believe me."

"What do you want?" I asked.

"Nothing. I just—I mean, I can imagine what you must be going through."

"It's none of your business."

"Oh, I know, and I'm sorry to bring it up, only—"

"Only what?"

"I wanted to—I had to tell you how brave you are. You know that, don't you?"

"Are you kidding? I'm not brave. I'm stupid!"

"Oh, no, don't ever think that. You are brave. I just wish—"

"What? What were you going to say?"

"Nothing. It's not important. I just had to speak to you."

"Why?"

The girl looked flustered. She shifted her books in her arms. Her eyes darted around nervously. "I can't talk," she said. "I just wanted to—to encourage you. Don't let those jerkheads at school throw you. They're trash. But you—you've got power."

"Power? I don't understand."

"Yes, power. Don't you see? Power to make things happen. Power to get out of the snake pit, power to get free. Don't give up. Fight your way out, whatever it takes."

"You're talking like—I mean, how do you know?"

Beverly stopped walking and gazed directly at me. Her eyes had a dimly familiar look—a certain haunted expression, like the dark, pinpoint eyes of a hunted animal. "I'm not as brave as you," she said flatly. "I wish I was, but I'm not brave." With that, she turned and rushed off in the opposite direction.

I plodded on to the Londerees' home in a daze. I kept mulling over what Beverly had said. The idea that she considered me brave astonished me. I was fighting for my life, that was all. Nothing brave about thrashing the waves when you're going down for the third time. I was just trying to survive—any way I could.

But one thing I knew for sure, and the realization overwhelmed me with a strange mixture of sadness and pity: Beverly was trapped just like I had been, and she didn't have the guts to break free.

16

It blew my mind to think that another girl at school was caught in the same agonizing death trap I'd been in. Maybe Mrs. Flynn had been right. I wasn't the only one. Now I wondered, *How many other girls were keeping the same dark secret and dying inside inch by inch?* Just as amazing was the fact that Beverly considered me brave for breaking free. I'd thought about it as a survival tactic, sure, but not a deed someone would actually admire. The idea warmed me, pleased me, gave me a gleam of hope that I figured might even see me through the rest of the week.

On Wednesday morning I told Mrs. Londeree I had to stay after school to make up an algebra test I'd missed during the hearing.

"Fine," she said. "Just bring a note from your teacher telling me that you completed the test."

"A note? Why? You sound like you don't trust me."

"Are you saying you don't want to bring home a note, Hallie?"

"No, it's not that. It's just that—well, maybe I'll take the test today and maybe I won't."

I was in a lousy mood as I trudged to school. I'd planned to telephone Matt at lunch time and have him pick me up after school. I was dying to see him again, but with school and the hearing there was never an opportunity to sneak away. By the time I reached the campus, I'd decided there was only one thing I could do: skip school and spend the day with Matt. I ran to the nearest pay phone, called him, and he picked me up before first period began.

"You gonna get in trouble for skipping school, angel face?" he asked as we headed back toward his apartment.

"Not if you write me an excuse and sign Mrs. Londeree's name."

"Yeah, sure. No sweat."

I snuggled up close to Matt. "I have so much to tell you. You wouldn't believe all that's happened with my folks and the hearing."

"Yeah? Well, you talk away, sweet stuff, but first I got plans for a nice cozy day with just the two of us at my place."

Before I knew it, the day was over, and it was time for Matt to drive me back to the school grounds. I hated to leave him. He was the only person I really felt close to. No one else loved me like he did. "You do love me, don't you, Matt?" I asked just before he dropped me off.

"Yeah, sure, kiddo. Why do you ask?"

"I don't know. I just wanna be sure. Today, it—well—you seemed—You won't ever stop loving me, will you? I'll always be your girl?"

"Sure you will. You can count on ol' Matt."

He pulled up to the curb, and I opened the door. "I'll try to get away on Friday. Maybe you can bring home some movies from the video shop. I just gotta keep one step ahead of the Londerees."

I made it back to the school just in time to walk home with Robin and Zena. I felt real smug over how I'd fooled everyone. Then Robin asked, "How come you didn't meet us for lunch, Hallie?"

"Oh, uh, I skipped lunch and made up that algebra test."

I figured I'd pulled the whole thing off good until Mrs. Londeree greeted me at the front door. "Where were you today, Hallie?"

"What do you mean? At school."

"Then why did the office call inquiring about your absence?"

"Uh—maybe they got me mixed up with someone else."

"No, Hallie, there's no mistake, except the one you made in skipping school. What did you do today, Hallie?"

"Nothing. I was upset about the hearing. I walked around."

"Are you sure?" Mrs. Londeree looked skeptical, uneasy. "Were you with your friend Matt Runyon?"

"No. Why would I be with him?"

"Listen, Hallie. If we're to help you, it's very important that you tell me the truth. Were you with Matt?"

I stomped on into the house and tossed my books on a chair. "Believe what you want. You will anyway!"

That evening there was an uneasy tension in the Londeree household I'd never felt before. I knew they were upset with me, and I knew I'd violated their trust. But I couldn't risk losing Matt.

At bedtime, Mrs. Londeree said, "Hallie, your social worker and I have good reasons for not wanting you to see Matt. He's nineteen, much too old for a girl your age. You've had so many traumas in your life, Hallie. Now you finally have a chance for a fresh start. You have a lot of learning and growing to do, but that won't happen if you hold on to a destructive relationship."

I bit my lower lip to keep from crying. "It's not a destructive relationship. Matt loves me, and I love him."

"But don't you see, Hallie? What you've known all these years isn't real love. Genuine, unselfish love is something that's still ahead of you, something very special that will come in time."

"Yeah, sure, OK," I said tonelessly. I wasn't in the mood for a sermon. No one—not Mrs. Wilcox or Mrs. Londeree—could understand the special bond I felt with Matt. He had been my rescuer, my protector. He would always be there for me and take care of me, the way I wished my father would have done.

"One more thing, Hallie," said Mrs. Londeree. "We'll have to set some restrictions on you for a few weeks. That means no visits to Matt, no phone calls, no contact with Matt of any kind."

I stared up at her in disbelief. "No, you can't. Please!"

"I'm sorry, Hallie. Believe me, it's for your own good."

"Yeah, that's what they all say," I muttered and jerked the covers up over my head.

I tell you, I wasn't in any mood to walk back into that hearing on Thursday. All I could think about was Matt. If I couldn't see him, would he find another girl? Would he stop loving me?

The preliminary hearing picked up where it left off on Tuesday—more crud about what happened, when and where, and whether I was the instigator or not. I was growing more teed-off by the minute.

Dad's attorney was going full steam ahead, knocking down everything I had to say. Man, he wasn't pulling any punches. "Isn't it true, Hallie, that you made advances toward your father, that you flirted with him, sat on his lap, and made sexual overtures?"

"Flirted? No, I never—not sexual, not like you mean. Did my dad tell you that?"

"And isn't it true that when your father rejected your advances, you became angry and decided to twist the facts, making your father the aggressor and yourself the victim?"

"No, that's not true. I never made advances—!"

"Are you saying you never wanted to sit on your father's lap?"

"I—when I was little—six or seven—yes, I wanted Dad to hold me. I wanted him to love me, but not the way you mean—"

"Isn't it true, Hallie, that you led him to believe that you wanted something more—?"

"No, no, I didn't! How could I? I was a little kid. I didn't know there was anything more. I just wanted him to—to rock me and cuddle me and care about me, that's all. Is that so wrong?"

"But as you grew older, your desires became more mature—"

"No, it wasn't me. It was him—his desires! His demands!"

"And in a hundred little ways you let your father know that you wanted a physical relationship—"

"I never did! I told him to stop, but he wouldn't—"

"No, Hallie. *You* wanted the relationship; not him. Admit it."

The room was spinning now, the attorney's words assailing me from every corner, taunting me, tearing me to shreds. I couldn't bear it any longer. I jumped up, sprang from the stand and assailed my dad where he sat, pummeling his chest with my fists. "I didn't want you to touch me," I screamed. "I hated it! You made me sick! I used to go throw up afterward. I used to lie in bed and pray that God would strike me dead before

150

you touched me again! How dare you say I wanted it!"

Dad struggled to his feet, gripping my wrists and holding me at arm's length. His face was ashen, twisted. "How can you say that, Hallie? How, baby? I thought you wanted it as much as I did. You loved me. How can you say I made you sick?"

"I tried to tell you, Daddy. I tried to—"

From somewhere I heard Mom exclaim, "What on earth are you saying, Howard? Howard!"

"Order, order in the court," demanded the judge. "Will the prosecution please restrain their witness!"

After Dad's unintended "confession," the hearing ended with startling abruptness. "The court finds sufficient evidence against the defendant, Howard Vernon Shay, to warrant a jury trial," declared the judge in his deep, ceremonious voice. "Jury selection will begin two weeks from Monday."

After we were dismissed, I ducked out of the courtroom and headed for the ladies' room to wash my tear-streaked face. I realized suddenly that Mom was right behind me. Her face was stained with tears too. "Wait, Hallie, I've got to talk to you."

I pulled out a paper towel and held it under the running water. "I don't think we should talk, Mom. We'll both just get angry."

"Please, Hallie, listen. How do you think I feel knowing it's all true? Just what do you think that does to me, Hallie?"

"I don't know, Mom. I'm sorry."

"It's like a knife twisting in my stomach. It's killing me."

I pressed the paper towel over my eyes. The cold wetness felt good. "It's been killing me for seven years, Mom," I told her.

"Oh, my stars! To think of it going on in my own house for seven years! You should have told me, Hallie. There's no excuse—!"

"I wanted to tell you, but you never listened. You were never there. I used to wonder why you didn't know. How could you not know, Mother? It was like a poison filling the whole house. How could you live there and not know what Dad was doing to me?"

"Do you honestly think I would have tolerated such a thing?"

"I don't know, Mom. I guess I'll never know."

Mom stepped over close to me. "There's one thing I do know, Hallie. Unless we stop this collision course we're on, your father will end up in prison. Is that what you want?"

"I don't know. I just want things to be different—"

"Oh, they'll be different, all right. We'll be in the poor house or living on welfare. Please, Hallie, you've already taken your father's love from me; don't take *him* too. Look at me. Would you just look? I'm begging you. You've stripped me of all my pride. Don't let them send him to prison. It would kill me, Hallie. I swear it would kill me!"

"What—what can I do? I have to testify. They won't drop the charges. It's too late, Mom."

Mom gripped my wrist. "It's never too late, Hallie. You owe this family something. You got us into this. Now you get us out!"

17

In the car on the way home, I told Mrs. Londeree, "My mother says it will kill her if I send my dad to prison."

"Hallie, you're not sending him to prison. If he's convicted, it's his doing, not yours."

"But if I don't testify, they can't convict him."

"Is that what you're planning—not to testify?"

"I don't know. I'm all mixed up. I don't know what to do."

"There's a very good chance your dad won't be sent to prison," said Mrs. Londeree. "He will more likely be forced to get the treatment he needs. It could be the best thing for him, Hallie."

"Treatment?"

"Counseling to help him take full responsibility for what he did to you, Hallie. Until he accepts the entire blame for what happened, he won't get well."

"But it—I mean, it's partly my fault too, isn't it?"

"No, Hallie. None of it is your fault, and that's what you have to understand before you can begin to feel good about yourself."

I smiled, pleased. "How come you're so smart, Mrs. Londeree?"

"I'm not. I've just talked a lot with Mrs. Flynn and Mrs. Wilcox. They both made it very clear that you're not to blame."

"Tell my mother that. She thinks I'm a tramp."

Mrs. Londeree looked over at me. "Actually, Hallie, your mother would benefit from counseling too. She needs to accept her own role in what happened."

"Are you saying she did know about my dad and me all along?"

"No, Hallie, but perhaps your mother let you take on too many of her household duties. Perhaps she wasn't there enough for you or your father."

I scrunched down in my seat and folded my arms across my chest. "What I don't get is, if they're both guilty and I'm not, how come I'm the one getting punished? Why is everyone rubbing my nose in what happened?"

"I don't know, Hallie. But you've been very courageous."

"Oh, Mrs. Londeree, I'm not at all brave. When I think about going back on that witness stand, I'd—well, I'd rather be dead."

Mrs. Londeree looked over sympathetically. "I know it's very painful for you, Hallie, but try to remember it'll be over soon."

"Yeah, sure. If it doesn't kill me off first."

"You worry me when you talk that way, Hallie."

"Then don't make me testify at my dad's trial."

"It's out of my hands, Hallie."

"You could talk to the judge and tell him how I feel."

"No, Hallie, I can't. The court won't let me get involved."

"You're just saying that because you don't want to help."

"That's not true, Hallie. Our family will stand by you."

I stuck out my lower lip in a pout and muttered, "But you can't stand by me in the courtroom. So I'll just have to figure out my own way to get out of testifying."

That evening I couldn't sleep. I kept seeing my dad's face in the courtroom and hearing my mom blaming me for all that had happened. I wanted so much for this nightmare to be over, but it looked like this was only the beginning. The preliminary hearing had been just a warm-up for the big event—a jury trial, with twelve strangers watching, hearing every ugly thing my dad had done to me. I couldn't endure it. There had to be a way out.

Sometime after midnight, when I was certain everyone had gone to bed, I slipped downstairs to the family room and telephoned Matt. I poured out my heart to him, recounting every excruciating moment of the hearing. "What should I do,

Matt?" I asked at last. "My parents, the Londe-rees—everyone wants me to do something differ-ent. I feel like I'm going to explode."

"I got the answer for you, sweet stuff. You pack your bags, and I'll come get you. Gordy's got a place you can stay. It's a little hide-away. I'll ar-range things with Gordy in the morning. No one—I mean, no one—will find you. What d'ya say?"

"Stay with Gordy? Are you kidding? He's a weasel, Matt."

"No, I don't mean stay with Gordy. He's put-ting up these girls. They're in the same boat as you—scared, alone, nowhere to go. Gordy felt sorry and took them in."

"I don't understand, Matt. I wanna be with you."

"Sure, be with me all you want, sweets. But not at my place. It's the first place they'd come looking for you, you know that."

"You're sure, Matt? I'll be safe at this place of Gordy's?"

"Come on, Hallie. Would I steer my best girl wrong?"

My hands were sweaty. "Well, if you say so. Just give me a few minutes to pack. I'll watch for you out front. Be real quiet, OK?"

An hour later, Matt and I pulled up in front of his duplex. It was almost dawn. The sky was all pink and golden, like a little kid had colored it with his crayons. The air smelled fresh and new, with just enough dampness to make goose bumps pop out on my arms. I shivered.

"Cold?" asked Matt as he lifted my suitcases from the back seat.

"Excited," I said. "I'm starting a brand-new life today."

Matt chuckled. "Yeah, you could say that."

We walked upstairs to the second floor. Matt set down my luggage, unlocked the door, and shoved it open with his foot. "Make yourself at home, sweets."

As I went in and looked around, I felt like I was seeing Matt's tiny, cluttered rooms for the first time. Maybe they weren't much to look at, but at least I would be with Matt. Or would I? What had he said about staying with Gordy's friends? Well, I would worry about that later. Right now I just wanted to feel like I was where I belonged. Matt would take care of me; he would love me always.

He took my suitcases to his room, then walked over to his little kitchenette. Dirty dishes were piled in the sink and on the drain board. "Want some breakfast?" he asked.

"Yeah. I'm starved."

He opened the refrigerator and peered inside. "Not much here, angel face, unless you wanna scramble up some eggs. We got ketchup. You like scrambled eggs with ketchup?"

"Uh, I don't know. I never tried them that way. My dad—he—he always likes his plain. That's how I always fix them."

Matt came over and put his hands on my shoulders. "Listen, Hallie, I'm not your dad. You

159

don't do things *his* way anymore; you do them *my* way, OK?"

"Yeah, sure, Matt. Show me where the pans are, and I'll fix breakfast real fast."

"That's my girl. Hey, we got corn flakes too. And coffee. We'll have ourselves a real feast."

As I broke the eggs into the frying pan and stirred them round and round with a wood spatula, I had the strange feeling I'd done this all before. It was like a shadow dream, with everything familiar and yet different: me fixing breakfast, waiting on someone, trying to please; someone else watching, judging, pulling all the strings. For an instant, when I carried the eggs over to the table, I expected to see my father sitting there. Panic knotted my stomach, until I reminded myself it was just Matt, my wonderful Matt.

"Hey, these eggs are great!" he said a minute later. "I didn't know you were such a great cook, Hallie."

"I've had lots of practice," I mumbled.

"Here, try the ketchup," he said, dousing my eggs before I could protest. I stared down in revulsion at the ugly red and yellow globs. "Listen, Hallie," he went on, eyeing me intently, "you and I gotta talk before Gordy gets here."

"Where is he?" I asked.

"Oh, he's over at the other place with the girls. He's got lots of things cooking, you know? I mean, big plans. A real wheeler-dealer."

"Doesn't he still live here with you?"

"Oh, sure. He comes and goes. That's why I had to clear it with him—you coming here like this."

My neck muscles tensed. "He said it's OK, didn't he?"

"Oh, sure, sweets." Matt's lips tightened. "Only thing is, he said if you come with us, you gotta pull your own weight."

I shrugged. "Well, yeah, I—I—what do you mean, Matt?"

Matt sounded a little irritated. "Pull your own weight, Hallie. You know, carry your share of the expenses."

"Oh, you mean, like help pay for food and rent and stuff?"

"Bingo!" said Matt. "You don't mind, do you, kiddo?"

"No, I guess not. Maybe I could get a job at McDonald's?"

"No way. They pay peanuts. Gordy's got it all worked out."

I put my fork down and stared at Matt. "What's he got worked out? You mean he's got me a job?"

"Bingo again." Matt laughed, but I could tell he didn't really think anything was funny. He shifted nervously in his chair.

"What is it, Matt? What kind of job?"

He leaned forward and reached for my hand. "You gotta understand, babe, it's only temporary. I'd never agree otherwise. Just until some other things come through for us, see?"

"What job, Matt? Tell me."

He gazed down at the table. A gob of egg had fallen off his plate. He squashed it with his index finger. "Hustling," he said.

I felt like he'd punched me in the stomach. "What?"

"You heard me. Hustling. Doing a few tricks."

My skin started feeling all crawly. I stood up and crossed my arms to ward off the sensation. Maybe I misunderstood Matt. My voice was as tight as a high-tension wire. "Are you saying—you mean—you want me to be—a hooker?"

"Just until we get us a little bread, Hallie." He shoved back his chair, came over, and pulled me into his arms. "It's not like I'm asking you to do something you haven't done before, Hallie. Only now you'll be making big bucks instead of just giving it away."

"I can't, Matt! Please, not that. Don't ask me!"

"Come off it, Hallie. It's all settled. It's no big deal."

"I won't do it!" I broke away from Matt and stumbled blindly to the window, my eyes swimming in tears. "You—said you loved me—"

"I do, angel face. I swear I'd never ask this of you if there was any other way. But Gordy says—"

"I don't care what Gordy says. Gordy can—"

"Hey, sweet stuff, can the high and mighty act," ordered Matt. His eyes narrowed menacingly. "Remember this. You're nobody. You're lucky Gordy even wants you. Girls like you are a dime a dozen, and don't you forget it."

I was bawling my eyes out now, choking back a searing disappointment. I couldn't even speak. The hurt just kept coming in rolling waves.

Matt's tone softened a little. "Hey, sweets, you look like a tiny little girl when you cry." He reached out and wiped the tears from my cheek with his thumb. "I really do like you, Hallie, but this is the real world, and what can I do? I can't change things for you. I can't make the world a better place. This is it. You run with it, or you get plowed under and someone else takes your place."

I finally gulped back my sobs, but I couldn't stop shuddering. Matt guided me toward his room. "Listen, Hallie, it won't be so bad. You come in here and put some makeup on that sad little face of yours while I go get Gordy. He'll introduce you to the other girls. You'll like them. They're not fancy broads. They're just ordinary, everyday girls like you."

I took a tissue from the bureau and dried my eyes, wiping off the smeared mascara. I didn't realize Matt had gone until I heard the door slam in the living room. I was alone. Then, with a sinking sensation, I realized I was alone anyway, no matter who else I was with. I would always be alone—whether with Matt, with my parents, or in a crowd. No one could take away this terrible sense of utter aloneness I felt.

I stared at my reflection in the dresser mirror. I hardly took up any space. When I blinked, I disappeared. Was I real? Who was I? Somebody? Nobody? A hooker?

"Hallie Shay, who are you?" I said aloud, shattering the silence. Impulsively I picked up the tissue box and threw it against the mirror. "And, what's worse," I screamed, "who even cares who you are!"

18

Fighting for control, I walked over to the bedside table and flicked on the radio. As I turned the dial, the room filled with sudden loud bursts of hard rock or heavy metal. I wasn't in the mood for those rackety sounds today, so I went on until I came to a soft, slow song. As I listened, the words stirred a yearning deep inside me just like the Sunday school songs the little kids sang:

> No one ever cared for me like Jesus,
> There's no other friend so kind as He;
> No one else could take the sin and darkness
>   from me,
> O how much He cared for me.

Swift, new tears filled my eyes. I sat down on the bed and gazed out the window. All I could say was one word, over and over: "Jesus—Jesus—Jesus." Just saying His name made me feel better, like maybe I wasn't really alone after all.

Was it possible? "Jesus, do You love me?" I whispered. "Will You be my friend? Robin says so. She says You're her closest friend. She says You died for her. And for me. But how can I be sure? How can I ever trust anyone, even You, Jesus?"

After all, I reflected darkly, no one was ever what they were supposed to be—not my mother, not my dad, not even Matt. Everyone had failed me. My dad had violated me, then refused to tell the truth. Mom considered me a tramp and blamed me for all our troubles. Even the Londerees were siding with the court system, insisting I testify. And Matt—my glorious protector! He was tossing me to Gordy like some old cast-off and making me do the very thing I hated most. How could I expect God to care about me when no one else did?

It was better, I decided, never to trust anyone, never to need anyone. Better to wall off all the wounds so no one could ever hurt me again. So it was settled. I was on my own. I had to depend on myself alone.

But I still had to find a way out, some way! Maybe I could travel to some big city—New York or Los Angeles—and just disappear in the crowds. I could be anonymous. No one would bother me or make demands or force me to do anything I didn't want to do. I'd be free.

But how would I live? I'd be broke. And who would give a fourteen-year-old kid a job? I'd still be trapped, maybe even walking the streets, just another loser.

But if I had some money—maybe Matt had some cash stashed away, enough to see me through a few days. I opened his dresser drawer and rifled through the junk. Socks and cigarettes and girlie pictures. But no money.

On impulse, I picked up Matt's razor. It wasn't the disposable kind. It had a real blade you could remove. I took it out and watched how the light glinted off its shiny surface. It was sharp. I held it against my wrist and imagined what a fine, quick cut it could make. Maybe this was my way out. No more running, no more hurting, no more anything. Just death and darkness and a long, peaceful sleep.

Was that how it was to be dead? An end of pain? No more thinking? No more feeling? Just nothingness? Or was death just another way of living? What if there really was a hell? Would I just be trading one kind of torment for another?

As I stared, almost hypnotized by that razor blade, a gentle voice came from a corner of my mind: *I love you, Hallie. I died for you.*

"Jesus?" I said aloud. "Is that You? Or is it just me, thinking—and wishing—?"

Something in the stillness of me said, *You know it's Him. He's waited all your life for you. He loves you.*

"No!" I cried, pressing the gleaming blade against my wrist. "It's a lie! No one loves me! No one!"

Even as I imagined the red blood spurting from my white flesh, I heard the quiet voice in my heart say, *Stop, Hallie. I've already paid the price. My blood was shed for you!*

Trembling, I dropped the blade and stared in bewilderment at my pale reflection in the mirror. Who had stopped me? God? No way! I jumped, startled, as I realized the doorbell was ringing. Was it Matt, back already with Gordy? But why would he ring the bell? I put Matt's razor back in his drawer and hurried out to the living room. Quietly I pressed my ear against the door and listened. Had the Londerees found out where I was and come looking for me? "Matt?" I asked cautiously. No one answered.

Finally I opened the door a crack and peered out. "Robin!" I exclaimed. "What are you doing here?"

"Open the door, Hallie, please," she begged. "I've got to talk to you!"

I stepped aside and let her enter. She glanced around, sizing up Matt's apartment the same way I had. I knew she was thinking it was a shack compared to her place. "How did you find me?" I asked.

"I heard you leave with Matt early this morning, so I looked for his address in the papers the Social Services gave Mom."

"Do your parents know I'm here?"

"No. Just me. But they've already called your case worker."

"How'd you get here?" I asked.

"We were looking all over for you and running late, so Mom lent me her car. She thinks I'm at school."

"Why did you come?"

"To take you home."

"It's not *my* home," I countered.

"For now it is, Hallie, and for as long as you want it to be. At least until things work out with you and your family."

I met Robin's gaze. "How come you didn't tell your parents where I am?"

"I wanted to give you a chance to come home on your own—so they won't send you back to Beatrice Crown."

I walked over to the couch and sat down. "I can't come home."

"Why not?"

"I just can't. It's too late."

Robin sat down beside me. "It doesn't have to be too late, Hallie. Look at all you've accomplished since you came to my house."

"Accomplished? What?"

"You've started a new school and made new friends. You're going to church and getting help from Mrs. Flynn." She hesitated. "And, even though it's hard, you're making a clean slate with your parents. You're making things right, Hallie."

I uttered a hard, little laugh. "Is that what you call it—making things right? Then why do I feel so rotten all the time?"

"I don't know, Hallie. Maybe it just takes time to change how you feel, or time for your feelings to catch up with who you are now." Robin glanced around at the nude pin-ups on the wall and the grubby clothes tossed over the furniture. "But I do know that this place isn't for you. It's not the answer, Hallie."

I sat back, spreading my arms over the back of the couch. "Wanna bet? I like it here. I feel right at home."

"What about school?"

"No sweat. I'll work it in. Somehow."

Robin's brows knit in a frown. "What about the trial, Hallie?"

I pulled my arms back to my sides and slouched down into the sagging, old couch. "I don't wanna think about it," I muttered. "And I don't have to—as long as I stay right here."

Robin wouldn't let up. "What are you going to do, Hallie?"

"About what?"

"Your life. Your future!"

I shifted uneasily. "Matt's got plans. He'll work things out."

Robin sounded almost irritated. "Are you always going to let someone else run your life, Hallie? First your dad, now Matt?"

"Why not?" I challenged. "All I do is mess up anyway."

Robin sat forward and looked right at me. "Listen, Hallie, you don't have to be helpless," she said seriously. "You have choices. You can decide what you're going to do. You're somebody special, and you have more power than you think. Don't you see? If you want to survive, you have to take responsibility for your own life."

"That's a laugh," I scoffed. "I'd only blow it like I've always done. I might as well take my chances with my dad or Matt."

"But they don't know what's best for you, Hallie. Only one Person loves you enough and knows enough about you to plan your whole life for you. He's the only One you can really trust."

"Who?" I asked skeptically.

"The Lord Jesus," she said softly. "I know it's true because I know Him, Hallie. Personally. I know what He's done for me."

I folded my arms and stared off into space. "Don't you get it, Robin?" I said with a catch in my voice. "It's easy for someone nice like you to be on—on speaking terms with God. But me—I'm not like that. Sometimes I do real bad things, things God wouldn't like."

Robin smiled patiently. "We all do bad things, Hallie. That's why Jesus died. He paid the price for our sins. He was the only One good enough. And what's really awesome—He beat out death! He came alive again. That's why His Spirit can live in our hearts now."

"It sounds real neat," I admitted wistfully. I couldn't help wondering if it really was Jesus' Spirit speaking to my heart earlier. No. Impossible. "It's just not for me, Robin," I said.

"But it *is* for you, Hallie," Robin insisted. "If you were the only person who ever lived, Jesus still would have died—just to save you. That's how much He loves you. He loves *you—Hallie Shay!*"

I stood up abruptly and walked over to the window. "You better go, Robin. I've got things to do."

Robin stood up reluctantly and sucked in a slow breath. "OK, Hallie. I just wanted you to know how I felt. I—I liked having you live with us. It was like having my very own sister. And Mom and Dad care about you too." She came over and gave me a quick hug.

"I'll always pray for you. Remember me, OK?"

"I will," I said as we walked to the door. Then I thought of something. "Are you going to tell your parents where I am?"

"I have to, Hallie. You're still in their care."

"I won't be here when they come looking for me."

"Where are you going?"

"Somewhere special," I said in a hushed voice. "A little island somewhere far away, where no one can ever find—"

My words were cut off as the front door swung open suddenly. Matt and Gordy came bounding in, laughing and talking at once. But they stopped dead in their tracks when they spotted Robin. "Who's this little doll?" demanded Gordy, pushing his stringy blond hair back breezily as he sidled over to Robin.

Robin stood absolutely speechless, so I said quickly, "She's my foster sister. She just came to say good-bye."

Gordy circled Robin, giving her his old evil eye. "Too bad. Too, too bad. She could give our girls a little class. Yeah, a real class act, that's for sure."

Matt stepped between Gordy and Robin. "Hallie says the girl's just leaving. We better let her be on her way."

"What's your hurry, bright eyes?" said Gordy as he sidestepped Matt. "How about you coming with Hallie and me to my place?"

I could see that Robin was getting real panicky. She practically lunged for the door. "'Bye, Hallie. I'll see you later!"

I winced inside as the door slammed shut behind Robin. *My last chance gone!* I thought wildly. But no. This was my life now—with Matt and Gordy. This was where I belonged; this was what I deserved.

Now that Robin was gone, Gordy turned his attention to me. "So Matt gave you the low-down on my operation, right, doll?"

"I—I guess so. But, Gordy, you know I got school and all—"

"School? Listen, doll, school don't teach the things you're gonna learn from me. Forget school. You're in the big time now."

"But I can't give up school. My parents won't let me—"

Gordy lowered his face real close to mine and flashed a cold, steely grin. "Your parents don't have no more say about you, doll. I'm calling the shots now." He put his arm around my shoulder and pulled me tight against him. "Now you listen real good, dig?"

"You're hurting me, Gordy," I cried.

"Cool it, Gordy," said Matt. "She's just a kid!"

"That's not how I hear it," Gordy drawled. He looked over at Matt. "You got a problem with how I handle my girls, man?"

Matt backed right off. "No way, buddy. She's all yours."

Gordy held me at arm's length. "Truth is, she needs a little polish and glitter, some flashy clothes, a new hairdo." He tousled my hair with his rough paw. "My girls will get you in shape, doll. Man, you gotta trade them Mickey Mouse sweats for something slinky." He steered me toward the door. "Come on, doll, let's hit the road."

I looked up pleadingly at Matt. "Are you— coming with us?"

Matt caught Gordy's gaze, then said, "Not this time, sweets. But don't sweat it. Gordy will show you the ropes. Just stay cool."

"No, Matt, please. You come too!" I cried. I reached out to him, but he just stood there looking sad and helpless, his hands hanging at his sides, the same glimmer of fear in his eyes that I knew was in mine. I understood then. Man, oh man, Matt was just as trapped and pitiful as I was!

Gordy shoved me out the door and pushed me toward the stairway. "Move it, doll," he ordered. "My wheels are ready and waiting."

I stumbled down the steep stairs with Gordy hot on my heels. When we reached the sidewalk, I could see his big, sleek black car parked by the curb. Then I noticed another car parked just ahead of Gordy's—Mrs. Londeree's little compact with the fish sign in the window. Robin was standing beside the open door, waiting.